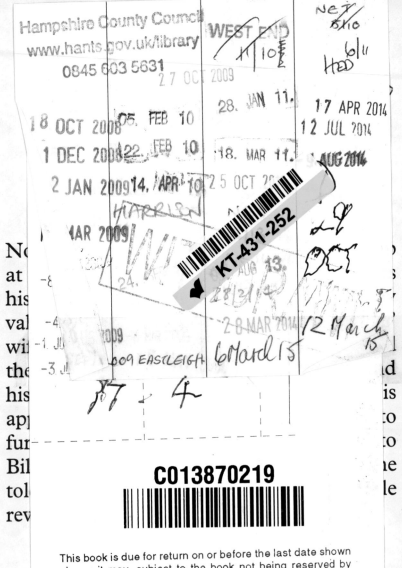

AVENGED

AVENGED

by
Julie Ellis

Dales Large Print Books
Long Preston, North Yorkshire,
England.

British Library Cataloguing in Publication Data.

Ellis, Julie
    Avenged.

A catalogue record for this book is
available from the British Library

ISBN 1-85389-633-0 pbk

First published in Great Britain by Severn House Publishers
Ltd., 1995

Published in Large Print May, 1996 by arrangement with
Severn House Publishers Ltd.

Dales Large Print is an imprint of
Library Magna Books Ltd.
Printed and bound in Great Britain by
T.J. Press (Padstow) Ltd., Cornwall, PL28 8RW.

Prologue

Bill Travers inspected his reflection in the mirror above the washbasins in the well-maintained Men's Room frequented by middle management executives. The reflection was reassuring. None of his inner turmoil showed through.

The tall, regular featured, charismatic young man who looked back at him appeared self-assured. Sure to be on top of any situation that might be thrown at him when he walked into his boss's office in five minutes. His Brooks Brothers suit, his Yves St Laurent shirt, mirrored the choices of Jim Sexton.

But he felt an edge of sweat circulating inside his shirt collar. Jim couldn't know about his near slip-up down in Atlanta last week, could he?

It was this damn hot weather. Always in summer he had to fight to hold on to himself. But in ten years, he reminded himself with pride, he hadn't slipped once—except last week in Atlanta when he pushed around that girl he had picked up at the Omni bar and taken to his hotel room. Hell, she was no better than a hooker. In ten years just that girl and Lynne. But his ex-wife didn't count; she'd provoked him.

It was always rotten for him in summer, he mentally reiterated. That was why he worked out at the gym, swam three times a week. *But nobody knew.* It was so easy to fool people. Christ, he was married to Lynne for almost five years, and she didn't know. Only those two up in Salem, New York, who called themselves his parents, *thought* they knew. They had no proof.

Nothing terrible had happened down in Atlanta. The girl was all right once she got over being hysterical. But he'd handled that situation just right. Even if her brother was a cop, he didn't want it spread across the newspapers that his sister had been picked up in a bar and went to the man's hotel room.

Bill left the washroom and walked down the long corridor to Sexton's office. He'd had a long talk with Jim on the phone yesterday morning about the business in Atlanta. This was their first face to face encounter since the Atlanta trip.

Sexton's attractive secretary, wearing a designer suit, sat behind a Chippendale desk. Rumour was that her chic wardrobe was company paid for and earned in the boss's bed.

'Good afternoon, Mr Travers.' Her smile was warm. That was good. She was regarded as an infallible barometer, indicating the Boss's current assessment of each executive. 'How did you enjoy Atlanta?'

'Marvellous city,' Bill said. 'Business was great.'

'He's waiting for you.' She nodded towards the heavy oak door that led to Sexton's inner sanctum.

Bill reached for the doorknob and walked into Sexton's Olympic pool sized suite high above Manhattan's East Fifties. From the tone of Jim's voice when he was summoned this morning, Bill suspected this meeting was important.

Was somebody in top management about to be axed? Bill resented Sexton Industries' steady pattern—like that of so many other companies—of bringing in top management from the outside. Why not somebody from middle management who'd proved himself worthy of this promotion?

Why not Bill Travers?

So he was young. Twenty-eight. With the company only three years. He had taken that machine that Jim Sexton created—through pure luck, not genius—and built up incredible sales figures. This year he was drawing seventy thousand. There'd be at least a twenty thousand bonus plus stock options.

He knew the formula that pushed a man to the top. Of course, being in the right place at the right time was a big advantage. The man who made it ahead wore the same clothes as the boss. He followed the same political line. He drank the same drink, indulged in the same sports. God, the hours he'd wasted on the golf course with Jim!

'I can see you were out on the golf course down in Atlanta,' Jim greeted him expansively. 'Great tan.'

'That's where I did most of the selling.' Bill was casual yet faintly deferential. Sexton always had to know he was the top man.

'That Georgia heat get you down?' Sexton left his chair to cross to the bar.

'Didn't bother me,' Bill lied. 'Everything's air-conditioned.' But it was a bitch to walk outdoors, even from hotel to cab.'

'Good.' Jim chuckled while he fixed the usual Chivas rocks. 'Then you won't mind Dallas.'

Bill tensed. Jim was sending him to Dallas? Christ, he'd just come back from Atlanta. But Dallas was virgin territory. A plum!

'Dallas can use us.' Bill played it low key. The way Jim expected. 'We can show them how to save a fortune in time and labour. In these conditions everybody's trying to trim down.' Don't push. Let Jim tell it in his own time.

'How's Lynne? Still working on the Great American Novel?'

'She's hard at it.' It was a miracle the way he'd managed to keep the divorce from Jim, but it was essential. Jim had built up this insane *schtick* about his so-called dedication to 'family values'. His public relations woman planted it in every interview. Everybody in the country knew: nobody worked for Sexton Industries who'd ever been through a divorce court.

Every six or eight months the Sextons invited them to their house in Ridgefield, Connecticut. The first time he'd said Susie was down with the chickenpox.

The second time it was a virus. Last time—four months ago—he confided that Lynne, with a degree in English literature, was taking a 'sabbatical'. *She's moved into a studio to get away from the hassle of running the apartment and caring for Susie. I've brought in a housekeeper while she's holed up writing the novel.* He'd tried to sound indulgent.

'And your little girl?' Jim never remembered Susie's name.

'They're both fine.' Despite the coolness of the air conditioning Bill began to sweat.

'Lynne may have to cut that sabbatical short,' Jim said with an air of perfunctory apology. 'I want you to move down to Dallas in two months. Set up a south-west branch. You'll have the whole territory to yourself. Plus a vice-presidency.'

'That sounds exciting, Jim!' He exuded an aura of anticipation. How was he going to tell Jim that Lynne had walked out on him almost two years ago? That made him a flop in the 'family values' sweepstakes. Damn the bastard! Envisioning himself another Ross Perot or Sam Walton. 'I always welcome a challenge.'

'Lynne will enjoy Dallas.' Jim approved of his choice of a wife. That was an

14

important part of the scene. 'She's great at entertaining, and there'll be a lot of that out there. Those Texans are big on parties. But tell Lynne the company will take care of all the moving. She won't have to lift a finger. We'll find you a house out there. You'll need a large place. And a pool—that's important for entertaining. And of course, your salary jumps. You'll need to keep up with all those Texans.'

As always Bill managed to maintain the proper facade while Jim expanded on what lay ahead. Top management at twenty-eight. A hundred thousand a year plus a big bonus and stock options. But unless he pushed Lynne into remarrying him fast, it would all go out the window.

Jim would throw him out on his ass if he found out he'd been lied to—that would be a personal affront. But he hadn't expected Lynne to go through with the divorce. He was sure she'd come running back to him. Damn it, he was a success. What more did she want?

Why did Jim Sexton have this hang-up about divorce being a sign of failure, a denial of 'family values'? Who in the middle of the last decade of the twentieth century considered divorce a cardinal sin? Hell, Jim wasn't even a Catholic! But nobody above the level of janitor worked for Sexton Industries if he was divorced. It would be a stain on the escutcheon of Sexton Industries.

Maybe he should have told Jim right away and tried to bluff his way out of it. But it had shaken him up when Lynne walked out on him. He wasn't thinking straight. It made him look bad, to be discarded by his wife. *He* should have done the walking.

Lynne had cornered him into agreeing to the divorce. He couldn't afford to have her tell the courts he pushed her around. The Franklins—those creeps who lived across the hall then—had been dying to testify against him. He couldn't afford that kind of publicity. *He couldn't afford any investigation into his past.*

'Before you leave for Dallas, I'd like to have Lynne and you come up for a weekend. Not for the next two or three weeks, but while the weather's still hot. We have the pool now,' he reminded complacently. A pool that had been charged to the company. 'I swim every morning before I head for the train. It's

16

the best exercise in the world.'

'I swim at the health club three times a week year-round,' Bill reminded Jim. He'd mentioned this several times already. The shrink had told him swimming was a good release for his hostilities. And he knew Jim considered swimming an important part of a fitness regime. 'Lynne likes to swim, too.'

He'd guessed Jim would invite him up to Ridgefield sometime this summer. That was why he went to Family Court after Lynne refused to give him weekend custody of Susie. So he could go up to Ridgefield with Susie and pretend the kid was with him while Lynne played at writing a novel. All at once he was sweating again. Jim would turn green if he knew Lynne was an editor at a girlie magazine!

Jim consulted his Piaget watch.

'It's getting late. My driver will be downstairs in ten minutes. I like to beat the traffic on Friday afternoons.'

At 4.20 p.m. Sexton left the office. Fifteen minutes later Bill emerged from the glass and steel office building into the torpid air of the streets. On this seventeenth day

17

of a record breaking heat wave humidity was a leaden lid on the cauldron that was Manhattan.

Traffic was horrendous. Passenger cars, taxis, buses, trucks moved like a film strip in slow motion. Anyone who could was fleeing the city. For the Hamptons, Fire Island, any available clump of shoreline.

Bill jogged ahead of a woman burdened with parcels and a Saks shopping bag to grab a cab she had flagged down. The cabbie shrugged while the woman swore. Bill settled himself on the rear seat and gave the driver instructions.

'Fifty-Eighth and Fifth.' He could walk faster than the cab would make it, but it was too damn hot. Heat like this set his teeth on edge. 'On the east side.'

He would go to F.A.0. Schwartz and buy a stuffed animal for Susie. Then home to the apartment to change into cooler, casual clothes. He'd drive down to Lynne's apartment. At six o'clock he'd be able to find a parking spot.

For the first time in his life things were going right for him. Nothing—nobody— was going to mess it up for him. He'd figure a way to make Lynne remarry him. She must be sick of that rotten apartment on Third Avenue. Her lousy job.

He'd pick up the kid tonight, lay some groundwork, then make a solid pitch when he brought Susie home Sunday night. After spending the weekend in the city Lynne ought to be a lot easier to talk to about their getting married again.

He'd sold himself to her before with no sweat, he reminded himself with rising optimism. He'd do it again.

Chapter One

In the sultry warmth of the corridor Lynne Travers struggled with the lock on her apartment door. Whenever she was tense, this happened.

'Mommie, I'm thirsty.' Susie Travers, three weeks short of her fifth birthday, lifted her appealing, pretty face to her mother.

'I'll have it open in a moment, darling,' Lynne soothed. 'What did you do at camp today?'

'What we always do. Margie had to leave right after lunch. Her father came to take her to the beach. Can we go to the beach tomorrow?'

'Not tomorrow, Susie.' The key turned over. Lynne thrust the door open to fresh heat. She'd close the windows and flip on the air conditioning. The living room would be cool in ten minutes. 'Don't you remember? Daddy's picking you up tonight. You're spending the weekend with him.' Lynne tried to mask her unhappiness with this arrangement. Bill had unnerved her when he went into Family Court to ask for visitation rights. She'd thought he was bluffing.

'When's Daddy coming?' Susie turned into the closet-sized kitchenette to help herself to orange juice.

'He'll be here real soon.' She had not been concerned that it took Susie and her so long to get home today. Bill was always late. That had been one of the myriad small irritations of their marriage.

Lynne crossed to the windows. The small living room of their Third Avenue apartment, near Gramercy Park, was furnished with modesty; but she was proud that no loan payments haunted her nights. No matter how much Bill earned, they had always been in hock.

Any minute now Bill would ring the doorbell. He would take Susie away for the whole weekend. It wouldn't be good for Susie. Bill would be bored out of his skull in two hours, and Susie would be miserable for the rest of the weekend.

Why couldn't Bill be satisfied to see Susie once a month for an afternoon, the way he had been doing? He had never once stayed the whole afternoon. By the end of two hours he always invented an excuse to leave. But Judge Erickson, charmed as most women were by Bill, gave him forty-eight hours custody of Susie once a month. From 9 p.m. Friday to 6 p.m. Sunday.

She didn't want Susie to grow up in the hostile, divided atmosphere that had been her own childhood. By the time she was three, her parents were divorced. She had been shuffled from one parent to the other until she started school. Then she lived with her mother during the school year and her father on vacations. When her father remarried, he'd demanded she live with him. She wasn't convinced that either parent wanted her. She was a pawn.

When her mother remarried, living with her new husband in the same town, there were split weeks between the two households. She knew of divorced couples who could manage to share their children with love. Who could integrate the earlier child into their new families. Her parents were too bitter at their first bad marriage; she was a constant reminder of their mistake.

When her mother died when she was nine, her stepfather sent her back to her natural father. When she was twelve, her father's second wife divorced him and moved with their child—her half-brother—to California. A year later her father accepted an engineering assignment in South America. He had never returned to the States.

Her father paid for her dreary boarding school and for college. She received brief, cold letters two or three times a year. She had not heard from him since his final cheque for tuition at the beginning of her last term of college. She had stopped writing after a year and a half because he never bothered to reply.

She met Bill during her senior year at college. He was a transfer student. She had been drawn to him from their first encounter at a campus concert. He was good-looking, charming, and slightly mysterious. Everybody was attracted to Bill. He had a magnetic personality. She had thought herself lucky when he began to pursue her.

Five weeks after their wedding she knew the marriage was a mistake. She was bewildered and hurt by Bill's mood swings, his sudden inexplicable rages. He was two men. She adored the warm, sweet, considerate man she'd thought she was marrying. She was afraid of the nasty stranger he could become in a matter of moments. But she was so in love with the other Bill that she kept telling herself she could make their marriage work.

When Susie was born, she was sure everything would be different. They were a family now. But it wasn't different. She was still married to two men. She stayed with Bill until Susie's third birthday because she wanted Susie to have the family she had never known.

Susie returned to the living room with a glass of orange juice and sat right in front of the air conditioner. Her long dark hair fell about her shoulders in silken splendour.

Lynne dismissed introspection.

'Susie, let's wash your face and hands and change you into something fresh.'

'In a minute,' Susie stalled, relishing the rush of cold air that encircled her.

'Now,' Lynne said.

With Susie's hand in hers Lynne walked with her into the bathroom. She washed Susie's face and hands, and changed her into a pretty, cotton pinafore.

'Does Daddy live far away?' Susie probed while Lynne manipulated the waist-length hair into a pony-tail.

'He's just about ten minutes from here,' Lynne soothed. Bill had moved out of their old apartment right after the separation. As soon as he realised every tenant on the floor was familiar with his temper tantrums.

'I've never been to Daddy's apartment,' Susie reminded.

'I know, darling. But you will today.'

Bill would drive down here from his place. He was a stranger to mass transportation. Lynne's eyes—the same Bermuda sea blue as Susie's, were troubled. Susie and she had never been separated overnight. Suppose Susie was scared? Would Bill know how to cope?

He had never forgiven her for backing him into the divorce, Lynne thought uneasily. But her sanity had depended upon separating herself from Bill. Knowing he was forever out of her life. For months she had penny-pinched to pay the lawyer. She had skipped lunches, allowed herself no new clothes. Thank God for the new divorce system. It had not even been necessary for her to appear in court. Mr

Campbell, the attorney, had handled the hearing.

'Mommie, can I call you and say good-night before I go to bed?' Susie's piquant face was wistful.

'Darling, of course you can,' Lynne reassured her. Susie was anxious about being away from her overnight. 'You just tell Daddy you want to talk to me, and he'll dial for you. I'll be home by nine.' Ira was coming at six-thirty. They'd go out to dinner, probably somewhere in the neighbourhood. They'd come back to the apartment right after dinner. She'd make sure she was here for Susie's call. Ira would understand.

Tenderness stirred in Lynne as she visualised Ira's tall, lean body sprawled in the leather recliner she had bought at a jumble sale in the building. He wasn't spectacularly handsome like Bill; but she cherished his quiet good looks, his warmth, his unassuming charm.

Ira understood she couldn't marry him until she was absolutely sure Susie would accept him as a stepfather. Susie seemed truly fond of him. Ira was delighted to have a ready-made family. He had a patience with Susie that, at unexpected moments, brought tears to her eyes.

She had been drawn to Bill's charismatic charm out of loneliness and a longing for someone who belonged to her. She had mistaken this for love. She loved Ira. She wanted to spend the rest of her life with him. And it seemed to her a recurrent miracle that Ira was happy to assume the responsibility of Susie. That he was already accepting her as his child. Bill was no more than Susie's biological father.

Bill was hung up on money. He wouldn't be happy until he was making half a million a year and wielding power—and then she suspected he'd look for more. Ira was a guidance counsellor in an inner city school and dedicated to his job. Ira and she would never have income tax problems, but they'd be a real family, sharing love and concern for one another. Bill would never be able to understand how important that was to her.

The intercom rang. That would be the doorman to say Bill had arrived. Lynne's throat tightened. She crossed to the intercom and pushed the 'talk' button.

'Yes?'

'Mr Travers is here,' the night doorman reported.

Even after living apart from Bill for almost two years she was tense each time they came face to face.

'Send him up, please.'

Would Susie be frightened when night-time arrived and Mommie wasn't there? She saw so little of Bill. She knew Ira better than her father. But Judge Erickson had given Bill visitation rights.

The doorbell rang. Lynne went to admit Bill. Clutching a huge carton he strode past her into the dining area.

'How's my gorgeous baby?' Despite the carton Bill managed to hold out his arms to Susie. She ran to him in a surge of affection. To Susie, Daddy meant fabulous presents. What had he brought her now?

Almost every month she had to chase after Bill for the inadequate child support cheque. He was drawing seventy thousand a year, and a hundred and twenty-five a month was a hardship! That and the cost of Susie's day nursery were all she had asked. Mr Campbell, the attorney, had thought she was out of her mind to be so lenient.

'Oh, Daddy, Daddy!' Susie's eyes glowed with excitement while she struggled to pull aside the wrappings. 'What is it?'

Bill took the carton from her and stripped away the paper. He ran a fingernail over the strip of tape that held the edges together.

'Something you'll like, baby,' he promised. His eyes swung to Lynne. 'You're looking beautiful. As always.'

'Thank you.' Lynne forced a smile. Hostility threatened to stifle her. Bill had no right to go into Family Court to ask for visitation rights. He'd never been a real father to Susie. He was too wrapped up in himself to be a husband or father.

'I'm in a celebrating mood,' Bill reported while he opened the box. 'Sexton told me this afternoon that I'm in line for a terrific promotion. Into top management. A vice-presidency and head of the new Dallas office.'

'How marvellous for you.' She tried to be properly awed. If Bill went to Dallas, then there could be no visitation rights, she recognised with relief.

'It's about time I moved up.' Bill was smug. 'Sexton knew he had to come across to keep me with the firm.'

Lynne disliked Jim Sexton. Bill had talked with almost vicious candor about Jim's womanising. He liked women in the kitchen, in bed, and making coffee

30

at the office. There were no women in Jim Sexton's boardroom.

The first time Jim invited himself and his wife to dinner at their apartment, Bill had gone berserk with excitement. That was a sign he was in favour with the boss. She had to rush out to buy Lenox china they couldn't afford. He insisted she arrange a fast delivery on ultra-expensive drapes for the living room. She had spent almost three thousand dollars—all charged—to make the apartment suitable to entertain Jim Sexton and his wife at dinner.

'Oh, Daddy! I love it!' Susie was enthralled by the oversized panda that Bill pulled from the box. 'Thank you, Daddy!' She flung her arms about her father.

'Susie, go bring out your overnight bag. I packed it this morning. It's on your bed.' Lynne strived to be casual.

The huge panda gripped in her arms, Susie hurried ebulliently into the bedroom.

'The promotion will change my whole style of living. A big house in the suburbs. A pool. Jim tells me he's planning to buy a company plane. We'll have two or three pilots on call. I'll be able to fly out to Palm Springs or Vegas for weekends.' Bill's eyes were amorous when they met hers. Startling her. 'You'll love Dallas—' Her mouth dropped in shock. *What was Bill talking about?* 'Lynne, it's time you got out of this lousy apartment. A big house in suburbia with a couple of acres would be great for the kid. Great for you.'

'I love living in Manhattan.' Bill and she were divorced. What was this craziness about going to Dallas with him? Nothing on earth could make her remarry him! 'Bill, are you sure you want to take on a whole weekend with Susie?' Lynne tried to conceal her soaring anxiety. 'Maybe you'd like to take Susie out to dinner and then spend the evening with her right here. It's comfortable with air conditioning on.' She was talking too fast. Her words tumbled over one another. 'It's so awfully hot outside—'

'Why don't you come out and have dinner with us?' Bill coaxed, the charm switched on full wattage. 'Then we'll come home together. The three of us. Lynne, the divorce was crazy.' He reached to draw her to him. 'We belong together.'

Lynne pulled away. She was trembling, striving for poise.

'I'm seeing someone else, Bill.'

She felt the intensity of the shock that charged through him. He was having trouble believing she could be serious about another man.

'You'll cost me a vice-presidency!' he yelled, and she flinched. 'Jim doesn't know about the divorce! He expects us to move to Dallas. He's giving me the whole southwest territory.'

'That's your problem.' She didn't have to cope with Bill's insane manipulations any more. *They were divorced.*

'Lynne, I'll move up to a hundred thousand a year. I can't antagonise Jim by telling him we're divorced. He'd throw me out!'

'That doesn't concern me.' Defiance swiftly gave way to unease. She sensed the vindictiveness cycloning in Bill.

'I was supposed to go out to East Hampton tonight.' He was backing away from the crisis with Jim Sexton. 'I gave up a gorgeous chick to spend this weekend with Susie.'

'You asked for visitation rights,' she reminded as Susie returned.

With eerie swiftness Bill's mood changed. She had seen this happen so often in the past. Later the ugliness would emerge, magnified a hundredfold.

'We're going to have a ball. Aren't we, baby?' He lifted Susie from her feet and swung her into the air.

Lynne started at the sound of the intercom again. Ira? But he wasn't due until six-thirty. Fighting inchoate alarm she crossed to the intercom and pushed the button.

'Yes?' Her voice was strained.

'Mr Edmonds is coming up.' George didn't even bother to ask permission to send him up. He knew Ira was the only man in her life.

'Thank you, George.' She turned away from the intercom to face Bill's hostile gaze.

'The Avon Lady?'

'A friend.' It was absurd to feel upset because Bill was about to meet Ira. Bill and she were divorced.

Lynne hovered nervously at the door. Why didn't Bill leave? He was making a point of meeting Ira, in his mind the competition. Underneath a show of roughhousing with Susie, Bill waited. The atmosphere in the room was oppressive with his rage.

Had Bill expected her never to go out

with another man? Never to remarry? Had he really expected her to go back to him after the nightmare of their marriage?

A chill darted through her. Bill had decided he needed her to keep up the image for his boss. Why couldn't Bill ever do the normal thing, Tell Jim Sexton that they were divorced? Before they were married, she had thought Bill was daring and original and exciting. Before she tried to cope with his unnerving mood swings. His belligerent inflexibility.

All at once Lynne was terrified at the prospect of Susie's walking out of the apartment with Bill. No, she reprimanded herself. She was being melodramatic. Nothing was going to happen to Susie. Bill was her father. He never laid a hand on his child. He beat his wife, she remembered involuntarily. Twice.

The first time Bill beat her, she left him. He pleaded with her to come back to him. He blamed the beating on his drinking. Drinking made him ugly. He swore he'd never drink again if she'd come back.

She remembered his alcoholic mother, who pushed him around when she was drunk. His philandering father, who couldn't hold a job. She remembered the little boy who went to school hiding bruises beneath his clothes. Four months after she left him, she went back to Bill. Seven months later Susie was born. They were a family. And Bill wasn't drinking.

But he had not been drunk the second time he beat her. Again, something had gone wrong at the office. All this time later she could remember him screaming at the dinner table. It was supposed to be a festive occasion. Susie's third birthday party...

'It's so goddamn hot in the house! Why didn't you call downstairs before I got home and insist they fix the air conditioner in here? You can't do anything right, Lynne!'

'Susie, time for bed.' She pushed back her chair. Susie was frightened each time Bill went into one of his ugly moods. 'Come on, honey.' With a cajoling smile she reached to lift Susie from the toddler seat attached to a dining chair. Only on festive occasions did Susie eat with them.

'Don't wanna go to bed,' Susie objected, taking her tone from her father. But Lynne carried her off to the convertible second bedroom that was her tiny domain.

All through the evening Bill bombarded

36

her with venomous insults. She had learned that silence was her best defence. He was furious that a cottage at the Hamptons was beyond their reach this summer. He had been counting on it.

Bill had borrowed to the full extent of their credit to have a decorator redo the apartment in a style that mimicked the taste of his boss. Jim Sexton said modern was cheap and crass. Antiques were in. Bill had nearly had a stroke a week before when Susie threw up on their new oriental rug.

Earlier than normal she escaped into the quiet of the bedroom, where the air conditioner offered comfort, and changed into a cool, short nightie. She heard Bill flip off the television in the living room. Then she remembered she had to go out to open the door to Susie's room. Susie hated to wake up to a closed door.

She was on her way back to the bedroom when Bill suddenly went berserk. He grabbed her by the arm, screaming invectives.

'Bill, you'll wake Susie—'

He punched her in the jaw. She staggered from the blow, clutched at the back of a chair. He pulled her free and threw her to the floor.

'Mommie?' Susie called out in terror. 'Mommie?'

'You goddamn little bitch!' Bill yelled, hovering above her while Susie cried out. 'You're no good! How many guys do you screw behind my back? How do I know she's mine?' His hand pointed towards Susie's room.

'Bill, how can you talk like that?' Lynne turned her head to see Susie hanging over the top of the crib gate. She was crying hysterically. 'Bill, let me go to Susie.'

'You'll get out of here,' he hissed at her and dragged her to her feet. 'Get the hell out of my house!'

He pulled her to the door and shoved her out into the hall in her flimsy, short nightgown. Then he slammed the door behind her and double-locked it.

'Bill!' She knocked in frenzy on the door. 'Bill, let me in!'

The Franklins had heard the rumpus and came out to bring her into their apartment. It was Mr Franklin who convinced Bill—in firm language—to open the door and allow her to go in and pack some things, and to take Susie with her. If he didn't, Mr Franklin warned, the cops would be called. Susie

38

and she had stayed the night with the Franklins.

For a while after that Bill was in intensive therapy. He insisted on giving her a full report of each session. Trying to convince her he could change. But he had switched from one psychiatrist to another. Never staying longer than three months with any of them. He never told them the truth. He bragged about 'telling them what they want to hear'.

'You pack your toothbrush?' Bill asked Susie, intruding on Lynne's ugly recall.

'Packed.' Susie's face lit up with a beguiling smile. 'Mommie thought of everything.' Thank God, Susie had forgotten that awful night.

Lynne pulled the apartment door wide, all at once eager for the reassuring sight of Ira. Ever since she met him eight months ago, she had known Ira would be special in her life. And he was so sweet and gentle with Susie.

'Hi, honey.' Clutching his flight bag Ira leaned forward to kiss her. Releasing her he spied Bill, stiffened. He knew the man glaring at him was Susie's father. 'I'm a little early—'

'Bill, this is Ira Edmonds. Bill Travers.'

She introduced them. Standing small and slight between the two six-footers. So different in appearance and temperament. Bill was dark-haired and dark-eyed. Ira sandy-haired and green-eyed. Ira's features were almost ascetic compared to Bill's rugged handsomeness. After struggling to survive in the path of Bill's volcanic disposition she treasured Ira's tenderness, his quiet control.

Bill ignored Ira's outstretched hand. He pretended to be occupied with Susie.

'Hi.'

Lynne fought against panic. Why had Ira arrived so early? He knew Bill was picking up Susie for the weekend. But he hadn't realised Bill would be upset at seeing him here. He didn't know that Bill was always late. Bill and Susie should have been gone by now.

Lynne saw Bill's eyes zero in on Ira's flight bag. His lips pressed together in disapproval. He knew Ira meant to spend the weekend with her.

'Did you pack your swimsuit, baby? We'll go up to the beach,' he promised, tickling Susie into laughter. But Lynne was conscious of his fury. He thought he needed her to keep up his image for Jim

Sexton; therefore, it was her obligation to remarry him.

'Bill, don't let Susie stay out in the sun too long. Not with that fair skin,' Lynne cautioned. Remembering the pool atop Bill's apartment house.

'I'll watch her,' Bill promised. 'She's just like you.' His eyes trailed possessively over Lynne. 'In twenty years she'll be a replica of you. Same sexy dark hair. Same blue eyes. Same great body.'

Colour stained Lynne's high cheekbones. It seemed obscene for Bill to be talking this way before Ira.

'Daddy, can I take him with us?' Susie clutched the panda, taller than she.

'Why not?' Bill reached for her valise. His eyes rested contemptuously on Ira for an instant, moved on to Lynne in seething rage. 'See you Sunday night.'

Lynne kissed Susie with an irrational sense of foreboding. She was becoming one of those neurotic mothers who was terrified every time her child was out of her sight.

'Be good, darling,' she told Susie. 'And have fun.' She turned again to Bill. 'Remember, not too much sun.'

'She's not exactly a stranger,' Bill

41

mocked. 'Remember all those diapers I changed? All the 2 a.m. bottles I gave her?' In Bill's mind he'd done those things. On rare occasions in Susie's early months he had played the helpful father. Susie had been a new toy. A source of momentary pride.

'If any problems come up, I'll be home most of the weekend,' she said. She recoiled before the vindictiveness in his eyes. He was sure Ira and she would jump into bed the minute he walked out of the apartment. He'd be outraged if he knew Ira and she planned to marry.

''Bye, Mommie.' Susie reached up for a final hug.

The door closed behind Bill and Susie. Lynne stood immobile, in a vice of panic. Why hadn't she fought the visitation rights? But Mr Campbell had insisted it would be futile to fight.

'That was quite a panda,' Ira chuckled. His eyes were compassionate. 'I'll put this garbage out in the stairwell.'

Ira made a small ceremony of gathering together the wrappings, ribbon, and carton and headed for the door. Stalling until he was sure Bill and Susie had gone down in the elevator.

'We'll go out to dinner right away,' Lynne called after Ira. She was impatient to leave the apartment behind her for a while. It was contaminated by Bill's hostility.

She hurried into the bathroom to brush her hair. Needlessly she retouched her lipstick. She could never be in Bill's presence, even for a few minutes, without churning inside.

'I'm sorry I showed up ahead of schedule. I wasn't thinking straight.' Ira was back in the apartment. His smile was contrite. 'I'm Number One on Bill's shit list.'

'It doesn't matter.' Lynne contrived a smile. 'He's Susie's father. He's not my husband.'

As soon as she could afford it, she'd drop her demand for child support. Her boss was such a bastard about raises. He knew she didn't dare quit and look for another job with Susie to raise and so many people being laid off.

'It's hot as hell out,' Ira said, reaching for her. 'Thank God for air conditioning.'

'I wish this heat wave would break.' She felt happy when Ira held her this way. He could blend tenderness with passion. 'Marty takes the energy crisis too seriously.

43

It must have been ninety in the office today, but the air conditioners stayed off except for one hour in the morning and one hour in the afternoon. Marty sprawls in his office in front of a big electric fan and gloats about how much electricity he's saving.'

'I'll be glad when you're out of that hellhole,' Ira said; meaning, when they were married. With Ira's support she could be more selective about jobs.

Marty Cole had hired her right after she left Bill the second time. She was to be editor for one of his sleazy girlie magazines. It was her first job since college, except for the period when she left Bill and worked in a boutique. She'd been scared to death she'd lose the job. Instead Marty kept piling more work on her until now she was editor of all but two of his string of magazines.

Her salary had not risen to match the increased responsibilities. Presumably her name on the masthead was sufficient reward. Still, it was a steady cheque. She couldn't afford to gamble on looking for another job in today's shaky market.

'I made reservations for an early dinner.' Ira released her. He sensed this was not a moment for them to make love. His sensitivity was endearing. 'We're going to Roma di Notte. All right?'

'Marvellous.' It was not a neighbourhood restaurant, but only a five-minute trip by cab. Ira meant for his evening to be special. Roma di Notte was their 'big splurge' place. 'Ira, this is going to be a great weekend,' she said.

But why did she feel so uneasy?

Chapter Two

Bill pushed open the door of the sun-roofed Peugeot and settled Susie on the front seat.

'We'll put this guy in the back. Okay?' he cajoled, taking the panda from her. All charm on the surface. Fuming inside.

That rotten little bitch! Pretending not to want him to take the kid for the weekend. She couldn't wait for them to leave so she could fall into bed with that bastard.

He had to go down to Dallas in ninety days with Lynne and the kid. He couldn't let Sexton know he had been lying to him. Sexton would throw him out of the company. This wasn't the time to be job-hunting.

Lynne kept saying she wouldn't remarry him. He couldn't believe it until he saw her with that creep. He had slaved for three years for this chance. And Lynne meant to ruin it for him.

'Daddy, I never saw your apartment,' Susie said with lively curiosity. 'Where will I sleep?'

'You'll sleep in my bed. I'll sleep in the living room on the sofa.' Lynne must have been on her back before Susie and he were out of the elevator. They'd be in bed the whole weekend while he worked his ass off entertaining the kid. They were having themselves a big laugh. 'We'll drop off your valise and go out for dinner.' He forced himself to focus on Susie. 'How do you like pizza?'

'I like it.' Susie giggled.

'We'll go to Goldberg's on Second Avenue,' he decided. He wouldn't think about Sexton now. Later he'd figure a way out of this mess. 'They have the greatest pizza in New York.'

With pizza, salad and a couple of

Heinekens, he'd feel civilised again. He'd be able to think clearly. He reached to unknot his tie, loosen his shirt collar. This heat knocked the hell out of him. Summers had always been a rotten time for him. But he didn't want to think about other summers.

Bill drove up Third Avenue, cut off to his Sutton Place apartment. He would leave the car in the garage. Goldberg's was a short walk from here.

He strolled into the ornate lobby with Susie clutching one hand. She listened avidly while he told her about the swimming pool on the roof.

'We'll swim tomorrow,' he promised while they zoomed upward in the carpeted elevator.

Lynne wasn't going to marry that bastard Ira. He'd kill her before he'd let her do that. He had the next ten years of his life plotted. He needed Lynne to carry it out. Right now Sexton was the big wheel, but he'd change that. All Sexton ever did was invent that machine. *He* was putting it across, selling to Fortune 500 accounts. Let Sexton invent. He'd promote and sell. In ten years he'd be Sexton's boss. Chairman of the Board. Not bad at thirty-eight.

'Daddy, can I call Mommie and say good-night before I go to sleep?' Susie was feeling misgivings about the weekend away from her mother.

'Sure, baby. If you want to.' Over his dead body she'd call Lynne. Let Lynne worry about how Susie was taking the weekend away from her.

He'd promised Sharon he'd run over and feed her three Siamese while she was holed up out at East Hampton. God, he hated cats. For an unwary instant the past threatened to intrude. Bill clamped the lid down on recall, as he had trained himself to do through the years. Sharon was one to make herself available on short notice. It was a convenient relationship. One not to be mistreated.

The phone rang while Susie was making a tour of the apartment.

'Hi, love,' Sharon drawled. 'Just checking to make sure you remember the beasts. In this lousy weather I wouldn't blame you for cutting out of town.'

'I would be at East Hampton by now except I promised my kid I'd have her here for the weekend,' Bill said. It wasn't cool to waste a hot weekend cooped up in the city. 'She's been dying to spend a weekend with me.'

'I've got nothing scheduled for next weekend,' Sharon offered in sultry invitation.

'Let's talk about it when you get back,' Bill hedged. He wasn't ready to think beyond this weekend. 'And don't worry. We'll go over and feed your menagerie.'

Susie had finished the apartment tour. 'Your apartment's lots bigger than ours,' Susie said. 'It's bigger than Uncle Ira's.'

Bill froze. *Uncle Ira?*

'You've seen his apartment?' Lynne had a nerve taking the kid there. *His* kid. Lynne claimed.

Was Susie his kid? Ever since she was born he had asked himself that at regular intervals. The obstetrician and Lynne had both put up a great show about Susie being two months premature. She had spent a month in an incubator at the hospital before they brought her home. That could have been a setup. Full-term babies sometimes weighed in at under five pounds.

Were Lynne and the doctor lying? Whose brat was she pawning off as his? Ripping him off for child support and that fancy nursery school. He stared hard at Susie. She didn't look like him at all.

'We had Mommie's birthday party in Uncle Ira's apartment,' Susie reported and Bill silently cursed himself. Again he had forgotten Lynne's birthday.

'Lots of people at the party?' He had figured right. Lynne was serious about that guy. She wanted Susie to like him.

'Just Mommie and Uncle Ira and me were at the party,' Susie explained. 'We had a frozen yogurt birthday cake.'

A cosy family picture. How was he going to handle this? He hadn't figured on this kind of complication. He'd known he'd have a hassle with Lynne—but he hadn't counted on her being shacked up with another guy.

'I'll change clothes. We'll go eat in a few minutes,' he told Susie and stalked into the bedroom.

In ten minutes Bill and Susie were en route to Goldberg's. The streets were hot and humid. No breeze. Wall-to-wall pollution. Bill opened the heavy wooden door that led into Goldberg's and prodded Susie inside. Cool air rushed to meet them. He took Susie by the hand and led her to a rear booth flanking the brick wall. Susie inspected the room with admiration.

'What kind of pizza shall we have?'

Bill demanded with a show of joviality. 'Chaste cheese and tomato, breath-taking garlic, sensual pepperoni?'

'Regular pizza,' Susie rebuked, giggling. 'Can I have a soda, too?'

'Sure you can.' Lynne's rules didn't hold up when Susie was in his custody.

It amused him for a while that Susie received admiring glances from fellow diners. She'd be a beauty when she grew up. Like Lynne. Fresh resentment pushed into his consciousness. What did Lynne tell Ira Edmonds about *him?*

He finished off three slices of the small pizza along with his salad and polished off two beers.

'You through?' he asked Susie, who was eliciting repugnant sounds from the straw in her glass.

'I guess so,' Susie capitulated.

'Let's go back to the apartment. You can watch TV while I shower.' How the hell was he going to push Lynne into marrying him again? *He had to do it.*

'You said we'd go over and feed some cats after we ate,' Susie reminded him.

'Later,' he stalled. So Sharon's cats wouldn't eat tonight. They'd survive.

With Susie settled before the TV, Bill

went into the bathroom to shower. Just the walk from Goldberg's to the apartment and he was drenched in sweat. He stood beneath the ice-cold needle spray and fantasised about beating Ira to a pulp.

He left the shower, tied a towel about his waist and went into the bedroom for fresh clothes. Susie was sitting practically on top of the TV, he noticed, as he detoured into the bedroom. She'd stay there until bedtime. He'd bring out a six-pack of beer and stretch on the sofa and read *Playboy*.

Back in the living room he paused in a sudden realisation of discomfort. Hell, the air conditioner wasn't working. He crossed the room to fiddle with the buttons. No relief emerged from the grills. He swore under his breath, kicked the air conditioner with one foot and swore again at the pain this action elicited.

It was Friday evening. The Super was off for the weekend. No chance of a repairman being available. Why did things always break down over weekends?

'Daddy, it's awfully hot,' Susie turned away from the TV to complain.

'I know it's hot!' he yelled. Susie's mouth dropped wide in shock. Don't lose control, he warned himself. The shrinks all carried on about that. Not that they knew anything. 'Go out to the kitchen and pour yourself a glass of cold orange juice,' he instructed, but Susie returned to watching TV.

He'd told Lynne how great he was doing with the company. *A vice-presidency coming up.* For a moment he blocked from his mind the reality of the situation. He churned with triumph. Then he was assaulted by the comprehension that he would never see that vice-presidency; Jim Sexton would axe him when the truth came out.

Why wouldn't Lynne come back to him? She was being a bitch. She enjoyed seeing him suffer. Because a couple of times he flew off the handle with her!

'Daddy, can we go swimming now? It's so hot.' Susie switched off the TV. 'My hair's all wet. See?' She lifted the thick ponytail to show him the moist tendrils at the back of her neck.

When she held her head that way, she looked just like Lynne. He restrained an impulse to smack her. Lynne told Susie to call that bastard 'Uncle Ira'. She was pushing Susie to like him. She meant to marry him.

'Honey, would you like to be real cool?' he asked in a surge of vindictive pleasure. Lynne was so proud of the kid's long hair. It had never been cut. It reached halfway down her back. 'Let's give you a haircut. Won't that be fun?' The prospect excited him. Lynne would be enraged. 'Come out into the bathroom with me,' he coaxed.

Susie's eyes darkened in alarm.

'I don't want a haircut.' One hand reached behind her to the silken darkness that cascaded down her back.

'Sweetie, think how cool you'll be. And you'll look gorgeous with short hair.'

'Mommie might be mad,' she rejected.

'Tell you what—' Bill dropped to his haunches before her. 'We'll cut your hair now, and tomorrow we'll go out and buy you the prettiest doll in this city. And I'll bet you she'll have short hair, too.'

'But Mommie might not like it,' Susie wavered.

'Mommie will love it. She'll be surprised,' he admitted, 'but she'll love it. Come on.' He took her hand in his. Wait till Lynne saw the kid with short hair. He wouldn't miss the sight of her face for a million bucks.

Bill led Susie into the bathroom. He

was elated at this decision. He dropped the toilet lid and settled Susie on the seat. Whistling he went into the bedroom to search for scissors.

'Take down your ponytail,' he called to Susie while he pushed through a dresser drawer. Lynne would be out of her skull when she saw Susie with short hair. *She'd asked for it.*

'Daddy, are you sure Mommie won't be mad?' Susie's eyes were fearful.

'She'll be glad,' Bill insisted. 'And when you've had your haircut, we'll go over to Sharon's apartment to feed her cats,' he promised. 'We'll stop off on the way and buy some ice cream at Häagen Daz to take up with us. All right, Susie?' He turned on the charismatic charm that was infallible with women.

'Chocolate chip?'

'Any flavour you choose.'

Bill stood beside her, scissors in hand. He would cut her hair so short there'd be no way Lynne could do anything with it for weeks. Her little darling wouldn't be so pretty. Lynne would hurt. She deserved it. Throwing that guy right in his face! How many other men did she mess around with?

'Daddy?' Susie gazed up at him in wistful inquiry.

'I'm just deciding how to cut your hair,' he alibied. 'Sit still.'

He began to snip off huge clumps of hair. Watching each cascade to the floor before he went on to yet another. Visualising Lynne's anguish when she saw the results. All Lynne gave a damn about in this world was Susie. Wait till that bastard Ira found that out.

'Daddy,' Susie said in a small, scared voice after a few minutes, 'you're cutting an awful lot.' The bathroom floor was a carpet of dark hair.

'I'll be through soon,' he promised, dizzy with exhilaration. Lynne's little darling wouldn't be so pretty with this new hairstyle.

He felt such power with the scissors in his hand. Susie's hair was as short now as Mia Farrow's when she did *Rosemary's Baby*. Lynne would be horrified when she saw her baby Sunday night. She'd feel sick.

It would be so easy to let the scissors slip in his hand. They were sharp. They'd cut up that pretty little face. Lynne would cry her head off if Susie had a huge ugly scar across her cheek. Lynne would suffer worse than if somebody had cut *her* up.

Bill's hand froze in midair. The scissors fell to the floor with a clatter. His stomach was churning in chaotic excitement.

'Susie, you'll get itchy with all that loose hair around your neck. I'll run a shower for you. You get under it and wash away all the hair—' His words were slurred in his agitation. He had to get out of here, quick. Before something terrible happened. He hadn't felt like this in a long time. He didn't want to remember the last time.

He reached into the shower and adjusted the temperature of the water.

'Take off your clothes and get into the tub. Be sure to close the glass doors before you turn the knob. This one,' he instructed. 'The water will come down just right.'

'Where are you going, Daddy?'

'To throw out the garbage.' His throat was constricted. His head pounding. *Lynne did this to him.* 'Get under the shower, Susie.'

Bill reached for the scissors and raced from the apartment, leaving the door ajar behind him. He paused before the compactor, pulled open the door. He threw the scissors down the chute. He was trembling, his face streaked with sweat. Yet simultaneously he was happier than at any time in years.

He knew exactly what to do to make Lynne suffer. He knew how to make her as miserable as he was right now. Knowing he was washed up at Sexton Industries. Everything he had slaved for down the drain. Because of her.

Lynne would pay for that. She would pay heavily.

Chapter Three

Lynne and Ira sat in one of the romantic, candlelit 'caves' at Roma di Notte. While Ira ordered, she tried to immerse herself in the charm and exquisite privacy of this area of the fine old restaurant. She was being neurotic to worry about Susie, she told herself. Susie was with her father. She'd be fine.

'You like the *Frutti di Mare?*' Ira sought confirmation when the waiter withdrew. 'And the salad?'

58

'Perfect,' she approved. The *Frutti di Mare* would be rich with clams, lobster, shrimp, squid and scallops. And the salad elegantly prepared.

'You're uptight,' Ira scolded. But his eyes were sympathetic.

'I'm always like that when I'm exposed to Bill,' she confessed. 'He brings back such awful memories.' Bill had made her his whipping post. He'd destroyed her always fragile ego. He'd killed her love for him.

Ira reached across the table to cover her hand in his.

'Stop worrying about Susie,' he commanded. 'She'll be fine.'

'She's never been away from me overnight.' Misgivings refused to abdicate. Why hadn't she fought against visitation rights? 'She's so little, Ira.'

'Bill will put himself out to entertain her,' Ira predicted. Determined to be optimistic for her sake, Lynne thought. 'Paternal pride.'

'I keep telling myself that. Bill can be so charming when he wants to be. Outside, among strangers,' she stressed.

Ira made a strong effort to divert her with amusing stories about activities at school. He had such beautiful compassion, she thought as she listened. Compassion and a sense of humour. When had she laughed with Bill?

Dinner arrived, and they ate with relish. The waiter came to the table to consult with them about dessert. Subconsciously Lynne checked her watch.

'It's just past eight,' Ira said.

She told Susie she'd be home by nine. Suppose Susie tried to phone before then? In all the excitement of spending the weekend away she might be tired early. Ready for bed before nine.

Ira seemed to read her mind.

'Why don't we pass up dessert tonight? Let's settle for coffee at the apartment.' His smile was reassuring.

Lynne was relieved.

'You're sure you don't mind?'

Ira chuckled.

'I don't mind.'

The waiter shrugged and removed the menus.

Twelve minutes later Lynne stood in the sweltering hall before the apartment door while Ira struggled with the recalcitrant top lock. Bill would have exploded by now. Ira persisted in his efforts. Unruffled and determined. Bill exhausted her with the rage that always seemed bottled up in him when it wasn't pouring forth like hot lava. With Ira she felt protected and loved.

'There it goes,' Ira said in satisfaction when the key turned over. Perspiration glistened on his forehead from the few minutes in the sweatbox hall. 'I'm glad you left on the air conditioning,' he said, prodding her inside the apartment. 'Wow, it feels great.'

'I'm sorry I rushed you back here,' Lynne apologised. 'It was ridiculous of me.'

'Next time we'll stay for dessert.' Ira pulled her to him. 'We haven't been alone together for a week.' His eyes and his hands told her how much he had missed this. 'We've never been alone here,' he remembered. Even when Susie was asleep, Lynne refused to make love in this apartment. They always went to his place.

'Let me get out of my dress.' Lynne tugged at the back, which clung damply to her shoulder blades. 'Then I'll put up the coffee.'

She cherished the prospect of a weekend alone with Ira even while she fretted over Susie's absence. By Friday of each week she was a mass of tension. Working for Marty had pushed a series of predecessors into nervous breakdowns or sessions with a psychiatrist. Being with Ira was what held her together.

Lynne changed into a turquoise multi-pleated beach cover-up that was a favourite of Ira's. While she hung the dress in the bathroom to air out, the phone rang. Her face brightened. Susie, she guessed with a surge of pleasure and hurried to the phone.

'Hello.' Her voice was taut with anticipation.

'Are you sleeping with that creep?' Bill's voice was a slap across her face.

For an instant Lynne froze in shock. Then she lashed back at him.

'That's none of your business!'

'You think every man is after you because of that pretty face,' Bill said contemptuously. 'But you won't look so pretty with your eyes swollen from crying.'

Fear spiralled in her. Why would she be crying?

'Bill, is Susie all right?' Alarm twisted a rope around her neck.

'Susie's fine.' Bill spoke in that unnaturally even, malicious tone that always warned Lynne of trouble. 'But you'll be crying before this weekend is over. Your pretty baby won't be so pretty—'

'Bill, what are you—' She heard a click at the other end. 'Bill?' Her voice was shrill. 'Bill!' He'd hung up. Her heart thumping, she dialled his number. She heard the ringing at the other end. He wasn't picking up. 'Bill!' she shrieked in frustration. *Why had she let him take Susie?* 'Bill, answer the phone.'

Ira hovered in the doorway.

'Lynne, what is it?'

'Bill—' She braced herself. 'He said, "Susie's fine. But you'll be crying before the weekend is over. Your pretty baby won't be so pretty—" My God, Ira, what did he mean?' Her voice soared perilously.

Ira was struggling to disguise his shock.

'Bill said she was fine,' he soothed. 'He's trying to frighten you.' Ira strived to be rational. 'You told me Bill has a sadistic sense of humour.'

'Why doesn't he answer the phone?' Lynne fought against hysteria while she dialled again. 'What's he doing to Susie?'

'Nothing,' Ira insisted. 'He's not going to hurt his own child. He's baiting you. I'd like to crack him in the jaw for that.'

'I have to go over there.' Lynne was

decisive. 'I won't spend the next forty-eight hours climbing the walls because Bill has a sadistic sense of humour.'

Her hands trembling so badly she had difficulty with the zippers, Lynne changed into jeans and a T-shirt and sandals. Ira sat on the edge of the bed and tried to put through a call to Bill. It was clear Bill had no intention of responding.

'I'm ready, Ira.' Fury blended with alarm. How like Bill to upset her this way.

'Let's go, honey.' Ira reached for her arm.

They rushed from the apartment and down to Third Avenue to search for a northbound cab. She would bring Susie home with her, Lynne vowed. Monday morning she would petition the court to rescind Bill's visitation rights.

Chapter Four

Bill tossed a change of clothes into a beach bag and added toilet articles. Damn if he'd spend the weekend shut up here in the apartment with the living room air

64

conditioner conked out. He'd take Susie over to Sharon's place. They'd stay there. He grimaced. They'd have to stay there with three cats. *He hated cats.*

He stalked towards the open door of the bathroom.

'Susie, you've been in that shower for half an hour. You can get out now—'

'I'm out, Daddy.' Susie gazed up at him in wistful reproach while she patted her tiny body with one of the oversized towels he fancied. 'I don't know how to turn the water off.' But she had carefully closed the glass doors.

'I'll take care of it.' Bill reached for a protective towel before venturing a hand inside. Lynne's voice ricocheted in his brain. *That's none of your business!* It was his business if she was sleeping with that creep. Sexton made it his business.

'Are we going over to feed the cats now?' Susie was hopeful.

'Sure. Let's get this show on the road.' The shower was turned off. 'We'll go over to feed Sharon's cats and pick up the ice cream on the way.'

He saw her reach with one small hand to touch her freshly cropped hair. She wasn't tall enough to see herself in the mirror above the basin. She wasn't going to start crying, was she? That would bring on one of his headaches for sure.

Masking his irritation he hurried Susie into clothes, ignoring her request to hold her up so she could see her hair.

'Susie, let's get over to feed the cats. They must be hungry by now.'

They left the apartment and went down to the garage for the car. Sharon lived on West Seventy-Sixth Street. On a summer weekend with everybody running to the beach or to the country they ought to be able to find a parking space.

Settling Susie in the car he inspected her haircut. She was still a pretty kid, but Lynne would die when she saw the long hair was gone. He reached for the ignition key.

How the hell could he save this situation with Sexton?

Chapter Five

Lynne and Ira hovered at the curb waiting for a cab in the early twilight. Why did cabs only appear when you didn't want them? Lynne asked herself.

'Susie's all right,' Ira insisted. 'Bill's accomplished exactly what he set out to do. Worrying you out of your mind.'

'There's a cab!' Lynne waved a hand in frenzy.

The cab zipped up to the curb. Ira helped Lynne inside. She gave the driver Bill's address and leaned back exhaustedly.

'Bill ought to be horsewhipped for putting you through this.' Ira reached for her hand.

'What did he mean?' Lynne persisted. 'What is Bill doing to Susie?'

'He's trying to upset you,' Ira reiterated. 'He's not going to hurt his own child.'

For a moment Lynne was mollified. But terrifying newspaper items plagued at her. How naive they were to assume a father would not injure his own child! The statistics on battered children were incredible.

No, she must not think this way, Lynne chastised herself.

'Bill never laid a hand on Susie,' she forced herself to acknowledge. More to comfort herself than to be fair to her ex-husband. 'Only on me. Only those two times.' She saw Ira's shock. His contained anger. She had never told him that Bill beat her. 'Even without that I couldn't have stayed with Bill.' She faltered. 'I was afraid of him. He had such violence bottled up. So many times I asked myself, how could I have married him?'

'You married him in a vulnerable moment,' Ira said gently. He knew of her lonely childhood. Her yearning for family.

Ira was close to his family. His parents lived in a small town in northern Connecticut. His two married sisters lived within blocks of his parents' home. Late in the summer, when she could take her week's vacation and he would be clear of his school assignment, he would take Susie and her up to meet his family.

When she married Ira, she would be

giving Susie grandparents and aunts, uncles and cousins. For herself it would be like being reborn.

'There were signs that Bill wasn't what he seemed to be.' Lynne brought herself out of introspection. 'But I suppose I wouldn't allow myself to see them. Bill had a way of ingratiating himself with everybody. All the students on campus thought he was special. He wasn't a particularly good student, except in languages. He spoke French and German like a native. But we were all convinced he had a marvellous future ahead of him.'

'He's successful in business,' Ira said grimly, 'but you have to chase him for a hundred and a quarter a month for child support!'

The cab pulled to a stop before the canopied entrance to Bill's apartment building. The street lights had come on. Night had descended on the city. Susie should be preparing for bed by now.

Fresh alarm clamped hold of Lynne. Was Susie trying to reach her now? Should she have left Ira in the apartment to cover the phone and rushed over here alone? But she cherished Ira's presence at her side.

Ira thrust open the door so that she

69

could scramble past him while he paid the driver. She darted to a glass-doored vestibule that led into the lobby. Normally a uniformed doorman stood on duty here. Tonight a hand-printed sign was posted, indicating the doorman would be 'back in five minutes'. He was on his dinner break, Lynne surmised.

She reached for the house phone, searched for the buzzer to Bill's apartment. Here. She pressed the buzzer. Waited with strained patience. Why wasn't Bill answering? She pressed the buzzer again, holding a finger in place. Did Bill guess it was her downstairs?

'He's not home?' Ira joined her before the door. 'He may have phoned from outside.'

'He's not answering. And the doorman's not here.' She pointed to the sign. 'We can't get upstairs.'

Ira tried the door to the lobby on the chance that it was unlocked. It wasn't. Lynne sighed in impatience, gazed out to the sidewalk. No other tenant was arriving to grant them admission to the building.

'I hope that five-minute break doesn't extend to fifty,' she said grimly. But she wasn't leaving until she saw Bill and Susie.

'Do you know if Bill has a front apartment?' Ira asked.

'Yes,' Lynne confirmed. 'Bill always insists on a front apartment. He'd get claustrophobia in the back.' She searched her memory. 'He told me he has a corner apartment.' To Bill that was a small status symbol.

Ira buzzed again. No response.

'He may not be home,' Ira pointed out. 'Maybe he took Susie out to dinner.'

'At this hour?' Lynne was disbelieving. 'Besides, he just called me.'

'He could have called from a public phone,' Ira reminded. 'Let's go outside and see if there are lights in his apartment.'

'He's on the sixth floor.' Lynne was breathless with anxiety.

They walked out to the curb and stared up at the sixth floor line-up of windows. The two corner apartments were dark. Every apartment on the floor was dark except for one in the centre. There the blinds were pulled high, revealing a pair of huge calico cats supine on the window sill.

'That couldn't be Bill's apartment.' Lynne was certain. 'He had a phobia about cats. Besides, I know he has a

71

corner apartment.'

'He might have taken Susie to a movie,' Ira said.

'It's almost nine o'clock.' Lynne's voice was unnaturally high. 'Susie never stays up past nine. She always conks out by then. Even on weekends.'

'We'll hang around a while and see if they show up,' Ira pacified. 'When the doorman returns, we'll ask if he knows where they went. Of course, it'll delight Bill to discover he's dragged you over here. He's trying to scare you.'

'Let's go to the police precinct.' She couldn't just stand by and do nothing. 'I'll ask the police to put out an APB on Bill and Susie.' Her mind told her this was irrational. The dismay on Ira's face confirmed this. Yet instinct warned her that Susie was in danger. 'I have to go to the police precinct,' Lynne reiterated.

'Honey, the police can't do anything,' Ira protested. 'You don't have enough of a case to warrant their taking any action.'

'Isn't Bill's phone call enough?' Lynne challenged.

'It was an ambiguous threat. I can't believe Bill means to hurt Susie.'

'Ira, you don't know Bill!'

'All right,' Ira placated after a moment's hesitation. 'We'll go over to the police precinct.'

Ira was uncomfortable about approaching the police, Lynne interpreted. He thought she was being hysterical.

'I'll go alone,' she offered.

'I'll go with you,' he insisted and raised a hand as a lighted cab approached.

Ira instructed the driver to take them to a neighbourhood precinct. He reached to hold her hand when the cab shot forward. Let Susie be all right, Lynne prayed. If anything happened to Susie, she wouldn't want to live.

At the precinct Lynne sensed that the cops had her pegged as a hysterical mother. The sergeant listened politely while she stumbled over the report of the conversation with Bill and explained her anxiety. His face was impassive. Then he sent them on to the squad room.

Lynne waited with Ira, struggling to conceal her irritation at the unavoidable delay until the detective seated behind a small, cluttered desk gestured them to the pair of just vacated seats. He listened to Lynne's report of the situation, then began to question her. He didn't believe this was a threat against Susie's life, she realised in exasperation. How could she make him understand?

'No, Bill never beat Susie,' Lynne admitted. 'He beat me.' Colour suffused her face. Why had she said that? She sounded like a vindictive wife, out to cause trouble for her ex-husband.

'Ma'am, I don't see that he's made an actual threat against the little girl's life,' the detective summed up. 'He came to the apartment. He was angry when he saw you were entertaining another man. Your right,' he emphasised, 'but your ex-husband was upset. He phoned up and tried to make you worry. He didn't specifically say he meant to hurt her,' the detective pointed out. 'We can't intrude on the visitation rights granted by the courts without a genuine threat to—'

'He threatened Susie,' Lynne interrupted. How could the detective be so dense? 'He said I'd be crying before the weekend was over. He said Susie wouldn't be so pretty. Does she have to be maimed before you believe he threatened her?'

'I'm sorry, ma'am.' The detective looked uncomfortable. 'There's nothing we can do. The father has visitation rights until 6 p.m. on Sunday evening. If he doesn't return the child to you at that time, then we can move.' The detective turned to gaze past Lynne and Ira. The precinct was short-staffed. Other people were waiting to be seen.

'He threatened Susie's life!' Lynne's voice was shrill in frustration. 'You listen to me, but you don't hear!'

'I'm sorry,' the detective apologised. 'This appears to be a family squabble. Unless there's an actual threat against your daughter's life, we can't take any action. If your ex-husband doesn't return the child by 6 p.m. on Sunday, we can go to the apartment and pick her up.'

'Lynne—' Ira gently pulled her to her feet. The pressure of his hand told her it would be futile for them to persist. 'Thank you, Lieutenant.'

In silence Lynne and Ira left the precinct. When they were out on the sidewalk, Ira tried to dissuade her from worry.

'You've overreacting. Susie's all right.' His air of confidence was meant to be reassuring. Why couldn't she believe it? 'But to make you feel better, let's go back to Bill's apartment and talk to the doorman. Bill may have said something about where he was taking Susie.'

They crossed to Third Avenue and vied with another couple for an approaching cab. They won. Ira gave the driver directions and leaned back to take Lynne's hand in his.

'We'll straighten this out,' he comforted. 'Bill won't drag Susie all over town. He'll bring her home and put her to bed.'

'You're being logical.' Lynne's voice was taut. 'Because you're a logical man. Bill isn't. He does violent things. The night he threw me out into the hall, he smashed every lamp in the apartment before my neighbours convinced him he'd better open up the door and let me get some clothes—and Susie, if he wanted to avoid a visit from the police.' Lynne knew the cab driver had become an avid eavesdropper, but she was too overwrought to care. 'At Westhampton one summer we gave a party at our rented cottage. He became furious at one of the guests: a man he had expected to become an important account. After the party he wrecked the furniture. The next day he called the owner of the cottage and told him it had been vandalised while we were at a summer theatre performance. Bill's capable of terrible things.'

'We'll find Susie.' Ira was firm. 'And I'll make him understand we'll tolerate no more threats.'

As the cab pulled up before Bill's apartment building, Lynne spied the doorman. He was standing out on the sidewalk. The lobby was not air-conditioned; he hoped for some relief from the heat by staying outdoors.

'Don't mention that we were here before,' Ira cautioned while he fished in his wallet. 'We might put his back up if we mention the sign on the door.'

'You talk to him.' Ira would be diplomatic. She didn't trust herself.

They left the cab and approached the doorman.

'Mr Travers, please, in 6–C,' Ira said briskly.

'I think Mr Travers went out.' The doorman was genial. 'But I'll try him.' Ira cautioned Lynne to remain silent while the doorman pushed the buzzer and waited for a voice to respond on the phone. In a moment he replaced the phone on the hook. 'I'm sorry. Mr Travers doesn't answer.'

'He should be home now.' Lynne abandoned silence. 'Maybe his buzzer isn't working. I'd like to go up and try the doorbell.'

'If he's not at home, I can't let anybody up,' the doorman said hesitantly, but Ira was producing the kind of greenery destined to change his mind. 'Well, I guess if you're friends of Mr Travers... But I'm sure he went out,' he reiterated. 'He had his little girl with him. Pretty, with short, dark hair and a nice smile.'

'Long, dark hair,' Lynne corrected. Realising it was irrational to be irritated.

'This little girl had short hair,' the doorman insisted. 'Real short. But she sure was pretty.'

'His daughter's hair is all the way down her back.'

Lynne turned to Ira for confirmation. He pantomimed silence.

'We'll just run up and ring the apartment doorbell,' Ira told the doorman. 'In case the buzzer isn't working.'

'Yes, sir.' The doorman's expression said he considered Lynne a weirdo.

Ira prodded Lynne through the much mirrored lobby towards the bank of elevators.

'He's out of his mind,' Lynne whispered while they waited for the elevator to descend. 'How could he say that Susie has short hair?'

'Honey, I suspect the doorman gave us the answer to this whole mess.' Ira was gentle. 'Bill told you that Susie wouldn't be so pretty. He meant he's cut her hair. He knows how you treasured it.'

Lynne stared at him in momentary disbelief.

'How could he do that?' Yet simultaneously she felt a surge of relief. Ira was right. That was the kind of sick humour Bill would relish.

They left the elevator and walked down the hall to Bill's apartment. Ira rang the bell. There was no response.

'Bill's cut Susie's hair. Then he took her out for ice cream or some such treat to celebrate,' Ira surmised. 'Let's go back to the apartment. Susie's fine.'

'You're right, Ira.' She managed an apologetic smile. 'I'm behaving like the classic hysterical mother.'

But why did she feel so uneasy?

Chapter Six

Bill manipulated the double locks on the door to Sharon's apartment and prodded Susie inside. He hated the West Side, though it was supposed to be loaded these days with creative people.

'Daddy, are we going to sleep here?' Susie questioned while he set down her weekender and the beach bag he'd brought along for himself.

'I told you we were.' He scowled and walked to the living room air conditioner. Flipped it on 'Hi'. He ought to be at the beach at some swinging weekend party.

'Are we going to the zoo tomorrow like you promised?' Susie pursued. She was wistful and forlorn now.

'Sure we'll go to the zoo,' he said. To shut her up. She was only five years old, but already she was pestering him. All women were alike. His bitchy old grandmother. His mother. Lynne. 'We'll go first thing in the morning.' *Don't start to bawl. That'll drive me out of my mind.*

'Can I call Mommie and tell her good night?' One small hand reached up again to her short hair. 'I'll tell her you cut my hair—'

'No. Don't tell her,' Bill ordered. He managed an air of conspiracy. 'Let it be a big surprise.' She wasn't calling Lynne tonight. Let Lynne worry. Let her lie awake all night wondering what was happening. She had to pay for what she was doing to him. 'Let's go out to the kitchen and open up the cat food.' He glanced about the white-walled living room with the red furniture that Sharon considered such a turn-on. 'Where are the damn cats?'

'Right here!' All at once Susie was euphoric. Three Siamese of varying sizes stared obliquely at them from the bedroom. Three pairs of exquisite blue eyes focused on Susie. 'They're the beautiful-est cats I've ever seen,' she effervesced. 'The Mama cat, the Papa cat and the baby cat,' she guessed and moved forward with precipitate haste. The three retreated. 'Don't go away,' she wailed, heartbreak in her voice.

'Don't worry. They'll be back soon enough,' Bill predicted, striding towards the long, narrow, windowless kitchen.

Susie trailed behind him, glancing backward at intervals in anticipation of the cats' return. Bill brought down the cans of food from a shelf, popped the first one into position at the electric can opener.

'Get that yellow plastic bowl over there and fill it with water,' Bill instructed. Irritated by the task at hand. But at least, the air conditioning worked here.

'Daddy, I can't reach the faucet,' Susie said after a moment. 'They don't have a step stool here like we have at home.'

'I'll get the water.'

The three cats were at the kitchenette entrance now, clamouring in a Siamese chorus.

'Oh, shut up,' Bill spat at them. He set the bowls of food down on the floor and went to fill the water bowl.

'They're so pretty.' Susie dropped to her haunches. Her face glowed with affection. 'Pretty, pretty kitty cats.'

Bill put the bowl of water down on the floor. He walked out of the kitchen and into Sharon's sparsely furnished bedroom. No furniture here except the queen-sized bed with a fake leopard throw and a small, black lacquered chest. He crossed to the air conditioner and flipped it on. Let the whole apartment cool off.

He flinched at the sight of Sharon's doll collection that was grouped on an avenue of black velvet pillows against one wall. He'd forgot about Sharon's stupid dolls. Dolls always reminded him of his grandmother.

He stood motionless. Staring at the dolls. Visualising another, far more valuable, collection. His mind was on a traitorous race back to his twelfth birthday...

It was a steamy hot Saturday morning in a small upstate New York town. Bill sprawled on the bed in his upstairs bedroom with the Sears' catalogue spread before him. He wanted a BB gun more than anything else in the world, but Mom and Dad just got sore when he'd asked for one for his birthday.

'Bill—' His mother's voice drifted up the stairs. 'Come on downstairs. Grandma's here.' From the lilt in her voice he knew Grandma was here with his birthday present. She was leaving this afternoon for New York to start on a cruise with some friends from her church.

'Coming.' Teeming with anticipation he threw aside the catalogue and hurried from the room and down the stairs. The English

83

racer! He'd told Grandma that's what he wanted for his birthday.

From the sound of their voices he knew his parents and his grandmother were having coffee in the breakfast room. He rushed to the door. His eyes swung about the room. Where was the English racer?

'Bill, honey, I'm sorry I can't be here for your birthday cake tonight,' Grandma apologised, fishing in her purse. 'But I brought over your birthday present.' With a loving smile she handed over a small, gift-wrapped box.

He gaped in disbelief. Where was the English racer he'd told her to get him?

'Bill, open it.' His father was faintly sharp. Dad was still sore because he broke that window last week. Not with a baseball, like he claimed. With a rock. Because he was mad at the Collins kid for squealing on him at school.

'Okay,' he said sullenly and peeled away the ribbon and wrapping to open the jeweller's box. He stared in disgust at the expensive watch inside.

'Don't you like it?' his grandmother asked anxiously.

'I told you. I wanted a bike!' He

deposited the gift on the table with a scowl.

'Bill, you have a bike,' his mother reminded him and shot an apologetic glance towards his grandmother.

'An English racer,' he hissed. 'That's what I said I wanted. Not that damn old watch.' He spun around and charged from the room. Knowing he'd figure out some way to get back at that mean old woman. She had plenty of money. Enough to go on a cruise. She could have bought him the English racer.

Late that evening he knew what to do to make his grandmother unhappy. He slipped out of the house when his parents had gone to bed and walked through the deserted suburban streets to his grandmother's small colonial house, set far back on an acre of land. The houses on either side and across the way were all dark. Everybody was asleep. Nobody knew he was here.

He went first to the garage and collected the axe. With the axe in hand he walked around the back of the house. Nobody saw him push open a window and climb inside. He went to the little room where his grandmother kept her doll collection and switched on a lamp.

A hundred and fifty-two dolls—insured for sixteen thousand dollars, Grandma bragged—were arranged on a series of stark white shelves. They seemed to stare at him through their huge, blue paperweight eyes. The pair of twin Jameaus that had cost the old woman a thousand. A wind-up Jameau that was worth two thousand by herself. Grenier No. 8s, two Bru, the Amelia Bloomer. The collection of Parian heads. He knew the names because she yakked about those dolls every time she came for dinner.

Methodically he chopped off the hands and feet of each doll. Then, one by one, he smashed those beautiful bisque faces into rubbish. Afterwards he felt great. Grandma would cry her eyes out when she saw that mess.

Nobody knew that anything had happened to the dolls until his grandmother came back from the cruise. Nobody could blame him. He knew Mom suspected him, but she didn't accuse him. She didn't want to believe he did it.

Not until the summer when he was fifteen and smashed up the old lady's house did Mom accuse him of vandalising

Grandma's doll collection. All at once he flinched. *He didn't want to think about that summer when he was fifteen.*

Pushing memories aside Bill walked out of the bedroom into the living room. Already the air was cool. Sharon's apartment was nowhere near as sharp as his, but it would do for the weekend.

By now Lynne must have gone chasing over to his apartment to grab Susie back. Wouldn't she be pissed when she couldn't find them! He pulled the drapes wide at the window that led out onto a shelf-like terrace. This was a sensational view. It would be sensational until they finished building the new apartment house across the street. So far the construction was low enough not to obstruct the view.

Bill returned to the kitchen. The cats were chomping away at the foul-smelling stuff. How could they eat it? Susie sat on the floor. Her head rested against the door of a cabinet. She was asleep. It was weird, the way she resembled Lynne. She was Lynne in miniature.

The old doubts began to boil again in him. Lynne was ripping him off for child support. Susie wasn't his kid. Whose kid was she?

A hammer clobbered at his head. He grimaced in pain. Damn it, the pills were at the apartment. He never had them around when he needed them.

He wouldn't feel this rotten if Lynne wasn't wrecking his life for him. Rotten little bitch. But it would be easy to get back at her. Now his mind churned with diabolic fantasies. A smile played across his mouth. *So easy.*

All he had to do was pick up Susie and walk out onto the terrace with her. Drop her over the railing. Fourteen floors to the sidewalk. And he'd have a solid alibi.

'I just turned my back for a minute, and Susie wandered out there and fell over,' he'd say. All broken up with grief. He'd been careless; that's all. The police couldn't touch him.

With a sense of sleepwalking he bent to scoop Susie into his arms. She was a featherweight. He walked out of the kitchen towards the living room. The terrace lay just beyond.

Susie would be dead the moment she hit the pavement. He'd telephone Lynne to rush over. Letting her know that something awful had happened—without telling her what. A few minutes later she would jump out of a taxi. She'd see Susie lying there on the sidewalk. She'd feel terrible.

Suddenly the phone was a jarring intrusion. Bill stiffened in shock. He broke out in a cold sweat. He stumbled into the bedroom and dropped Susie onto the bed. That damn noise made his headache worse. He picked up the phone and let it fall to the floor.

'Hello? Hello?' A feminine voice at the other end was exasperated. One of Sharon's kooky girlfriends. 'What's going on there? Hey!'

Pick it up and answer before that slut called the cops. She might decide somebody had broken into the apartment. He bent to retrieve the phone.

'Sharon's not home. I'm here to feed the cats,' he said brusquely. 'Call her Sunday night.'

He slammed the phone back on the hook and went out into the living room. His hands were shaking. His stomach was on a roller coaster. One of the cats brushed up against him. Siamese were too damn noisy. He stared down at the cat. It was the one Susie called 'the Mama cat'. Rotten little bitch.

His face contorted with contempt Bill

picked up the cat and went out onto the terrace. The cat yowled in reproach. His hand was a vice about its fragile body.

He lifted the cat over the railing. He watched while she fell to the sidewalk. A spattering of beige fur and blood. One less bitch in this world.

Chapter Seven

In the damp, cool comfort of the bedroom air conditioning, Lynne lay sleepless. She had tried to reach Bill a dozen times before Ira insisted she make an effort to get some sleep. Bill was deliberately keeping Susie from her.

Where were they? At somebody's beach house, the way Ira suspected? At a motel in Westchester or Connecticut? Bill was paranoid about the heat, she recalled.

She comprehended the logic in Ira's conviction that Susie's haircut was what Bill meant when he phoned her with that strangely couched threat. For a little while she had been able to relax in the solace of Ira's arms. But now logic was losing out to instinct.

She thrust aside the flower-splashed sheet and slid her feet to the floor. Ira was asleep. In the faint light that seeped through the Venetian blinds she walked on cat-quiet feet from the bedroom into the living room. Careful to close the door behind her to contain the bedroom air conditioning for Ira's comfort.

With no mechanical relief the living room air was oppressive and stale. Lynne crossed to a window and tugged it open several inches. For a few moments she gazed into the sultry, grey dawn while the drone of endless air conditioners assaulted her ears.

The street below was deserted except for a strident sanitation truck. An occasional car moved along Third Avenue. She spied the white and blue of a police car and winced. Despite logic she was scared. Where was Susie right this minute? Was she sleeping well? Was she frightened?

Yesterday's heat continued to lay heavy on the city. Lynne closed the window again. Flipped on the living room air conditioner. The Con. Ed. bill this month would be a horror, but she couldn't cope tonight with this weather.

Why hadn't Bill stayed at the apartment? Then she wouldn't be living in a nightmare. But Bill didn't want her to be able to reach him, her mind pinpointed again. Bill acquired malicious pleasure from making her suffer.

'Lynne?' Ira's voice seemed unnaturally loud in the night stillness.

Lynne swung around with a contrite smile.

'I didn't meant to wake you.'

'You didn't wake me,' he contradicted. His smile was meant to be reassuring. 'It was that awful garbage truck. Why can't they pick up at civilised hours?'

'Ira, if I could know where Susie is!' Lynne burst out in desperation. 'If I could be sure she's all right.' Self-recriminations ripped at her again. 'It's my fault she's with Bill. I should have fought against the visitation rights. Why did Mr Campbell insist that I let it ride?'

'Granting visitation rights to the father is a common practice,' Ira reminded. 'Millions of fathers have this.'

'Millions of fathers are not like Bill.' Her face tensed. 'I should have fought it.'

'Lynne, you couldn't have stopped the Judge from giving Bill visitation rights. He comes over as a responsible, intelligent man. He holds a substantial job. He's never been violent towards Susie. She's never shown any fear towards him. You told me she's always happy to see him.'

'He always comes with a present.' Lynne shook her head in defeat. 'He wins her over. She's forgotten that night when she hung over the crib gate screaming in terror while she watched him beat me. For over a year she had nightmares. I'd wake her and take her into bed with me. She'd sleep for the rest of the night with her arms around my neck. But now she associates Bill with presents,' Lynne said bitterly. She'd prayed that Susie would never be aware of hostility between her parents. She wanted to spare her child what she had suffered.

'Honey, it's better that she forgot.'

'It's funny. A lot of people who knew us were shocked when I walked out on Bill. Except the tenants on our floor who had heard him carry on.' Lynne was imprisoned for a moment in painful recall. 'Everybody else was sure I'd lost my mind. Here was this handsome, successful husband, who made a point of charming everybody. They didn't know he made me his whipping post. They wouldn't believe me if I tried to tell them Bill's potential for violence.'

'A lot of people have that potential.' Ira's face was sombre. 'But it only surfaces under special provocation.'

'Ira, I gave him that provocation. I let him discover I was in love with another man. He expected to push me into remarrying him. He considers that crucial to his career. He's convinced Jim Sexton will throw him out of the company if he finds out we're divorced.'

'Lynne, that's insane,' Ira rejected. 'Perhaps fifty years ago, but today?'

'It's not insane,' Lynne capitulated tiredly. 'Jim Sexton is a tyrant. Every member of the firm who's ever been involved in a divorce has been fired. Not many of the employees know this, but one of the wives told me at one of their cocktail parties that both his wife and he are die-hard Catholics. He wishes he could divorce his wife. The Church says he can't. If he can't, then nobody in his employ can have that option. Bill's scheduled to open up a Dallas office. It's a tremendous promotion. A vice-presidency. But when Sexton discovers that Bill has lied to him and we're divorced, Bill's through with Sexton Industries.'

'But if Bill's worth so much to the company—' Ira was puzzled.

'Nobody's worth that much.'

Lynne shivered as she envisioned Bill's rage when he was forced into a confrontation with Jim Sexton. She had left him because she was terrified of those rages. She was afraid that one day he might kill her.

In the torpid stillness of the night Lynne's mind acquired a new clarity. She grappled with the reality she had managed to avoid in the years she lived with Bill. Her former husband was a psychotic. *And her baby was alone with him.*

Chapter Eight

Bill turned off the 1949 flick at 5.53 a.m. and went out to the kitchen for the last of the six-pack Sharon had stashed in the fridge for him. For a few hours beer and the tube blurred the disaster that waited to demolish him. Always he had a way of circling around the object of his rage, like some jungle animal revving up for the kill.

With the last can of beer in his hand he returned to the living room sofa. What a bitch of a Friday night! He ought to be sacked out with some great chick. He could walk into any singles bar and have his choice. Instead, he was stuck here in this crummy apartment playing nursemaid to a kid being pushed off as his.

Now his mind took a swat at reality. He had screwed himself by lying to Jim. But how could he have done anything else? He had been sparring for time. By now Lynne should have been ready to remarry him. Hadn't she had enough of that rotten job? But he hadn't counted on her throwing herself at another guy.

At the top management level a man had to have a wife. The *right* wife. In Dallas he'd have to entertain regularly. That was big in Texas. Lynne didn't give a shit about what she did to his career. She'd forgot about all he had done for her. He married her when she had nobody to turn to; but when he needed her, she was screwing that asshole Ira.

Was Lynne lying in bed with Ira right this minute? The two of them laughing about how they'd pushed the kid off on him? She wasn't even his kid. He'd known that almost from the minute Lynne told him she was pregnant.

Lynne and the doctor were in cahoots to make him believe she was carrying his baby. They knew they'd have to make it look as though Susie was a preemie. Lynne and he had been separated for four months—and then, zingo, seven months later she gave birth to Susie.

All that shit about Susie being a preemie! The doctor would have said anything Lynne asked him to say. He'd had the hots for Lynne all through her pregnancy.

Maybe they'd been having a thing those four months she was away. All of a sudden he clutched at a fresh supposition. *That's why she came back.* Because she was pregnant with the doctor's baby.

In an explosive burst of anger Bill left the sofa and crossed to the telephone. He dialled. He could hear the ringing at the other end. Once. Twice. Three times. Why in hell didn't Lynne pick up?

Chapter Nine

Lynne awoke with a start. Exhausted, she had fallen asleep an hour before. The sound of the phone ringing was a raucous intrusion. She fumbled towards the night table, struggling into a half-sitting position as she brought the receiver to her ear.

'Hello—' Simultaneously her eyes focused on the clock. It was 6.05 a.m.

'Did you sleep well last night?' Bill asked in the menacing monotone she had learned to fear.

'Bill, where are you?' Her heart was pounding. 'Where's Susie? Let me talk to her!'

'I slept well.' It was as though Bill had not heard her. As though he carried on a monologue. 'Susie slept well. Last night she slept well.' An insidious threat sneaked into his voice.

'Bill, let me talk to her!' Terror lent a sharpness to her voice. But Bill didn't seem to hear her.

'Susie's still pretty. She would have

grown up to look just like you.' All at once the atmosphere was suffocating. 'Susie won't be pretty with an arm chewed off, will she? Remember when we read about that little girl in Yosemite National Park? Or was it Yellowstone? It was in all the newspapers.'

'Bill, what are you talking about?' Lynne fought against hysteria. *He meant to maim Susie. His own child. She had to stop him.* 'Where's Susie?'

'You rotten bitch!' he lashed at her. 'You're making me look bad before Jim Sexton! You're costing me a vice-presidency. You shouldn't have done that, Lynne.' She heard the harsh click of the phone at the other end.

'Bill, wait!' she pleaded. The phone was dead. 'Bill!'

'What did he say?' Ira was awake. Calculatingly calm.

'More of the same.' Bill was Susie's father. How could he behave this way? 'He said, "She's still pretty." Then he talked about that little girl a few years ago, who had an arm chewed off in some national park. Ira, this is unreal—'

'He wouldn't say where they are?'

'I don't think he even heard me. Ira, I

99

must go back to the police precinct. They'll have to listen to me now. I'll insist they put a tap in this line. We'll discover where Bill's calling from!'

'He's off the phone too fast for them to trace the call. Besides, they still can't take any action. He hasn't spelled out any real threat. He's ambiguous.' Ira managed a wry smile. 'A wire tap would be violating Bill's civil liberties.'

'I know what Bill's saying!' Panic drained her face of colour. 'He's threatening to maim Susie to get back at me. Ira, he's psychotic!' How many times had that suspicion loomed in her mind? Each time she had told herself she was being melodramatic. Bill was short-tempered and irascible. Nothing more. But she could no longer delude herself into believing that.

'Bill's out to scare the hell out of you, and he's succeeding.' Ira was grim. 'The police can't put out an APB on the strength of what's happened. Bill must be aware of that.'

'Am I supposed to wait until he brings Susie home to me in God knows what condition?' Lynne's voice broke. '*Then* the police will take action?'

Ira flinched before the accusation in her eyes.

'The police can't take action. But we can.' All at once he was decisive. 'We'll call your lawyer. Let Campbell advise us.' Though Ira seemed calm, Lynne was sensing his anxiety. 'We can't phone this early. We'll wait until eight,' he compromised. 'Then we'll explain it's an emergency.'

'Ira, this is bizarre.' Lynne shook her head in bewilderment. 'The police should go after Bill.'

'The law is on his side.' Ira struggled not to show his apprehension, but Lynne sensed it. 'There's only one chance in a million that Bill will try to hurt Susie.'

'I have no gambling instinct. Not when the stake is my child. I must find Susie before Bill does something horrible.' But how was she to find her without the police? What could Mr Campbell tell them?

'Let's try to be logical. Try to get inside Bill's head. Let's go back to that business about the bear,' Ira said, and Lynne shuddered. 'Would Bill take Susie to the zoo?'

She stared at him in relief.

'Oh, Ira, yes!'

'The Bronx Zoo? The Central Park Zoo?' Ira probed.

'The Central Park Zoo. She loves it. I've taken her there often. Do you think that's what Bill meant? He's taking her to the zoo?' Lynne clung to this possibility. 'Ira, let's be there waiting for him. I don't care what I have to do. I'm bringing Susie home with me. To the devil with the Court. I won't let her stay with Bill.'

'What time does the zoo open? Do they have special hours on Saturdays?'

'They open every day at 10 a.m. Susie and I were there twice last month.' Lynne's mind rushed ahead. 'It's not far from Bill's apartment. He must be taking her there today!'

She visualised the polar bears at the zoo. Huge and restless in this steamy weather. But nothing could happen to Susie at the Central Park Zoo. Not with those tall, glass enclosures. *Could it?*

'You'll phone Campbell at eight,' Ira plotted. 'We'll hear what he advises. But by ten we'll be at the zoo.' He rose from the bed. 'Go take a shower and dress. I'll make some coffee.'

'I can't believe this is happening.' This was some awful nightmare. Some horror film they were watching on TV. It couldn't be happening. But she was here with Ira—and Susie was somewhere with Bill.

'It's going to be all right,' Ira promised. 'Just hang in there.'

Lynne's eyes clung to the clock. It was 8 a.m.: time to call Mr Campbell. She reached for the telephone—the fourth cup of coffee of the morning at hand—and dialled Campbell's house number, given to her earlier in the event of an emergency during the divorce period. Her shoulders ached with tension. It seemed as though Ira and she had been awake for a dozen hours.

She geared herself for the lawyer's annoyance at being called at this hour on a Saturday morning. Dear God, let him be home.

To her astonishment the phone was picked up on the first ring.

'Hello.' A woman answered. Crisp and polite.

'May I speak to Mr Campbell, please.'

'Who is this?' The woman at the other end was wary.

'I'm a client of Mr Campbell's. Lynne Travers. I'm sorry to call so early,' she

103

apologised, 'but this is an emergency.'

'Just a moment.'

Lynne's heart pounded. Perhaps Mr Campbell would know how to propel the police onto Bill's trail. There must be a way the police could intervene.

'Yes, Mrs Travers?' Campbell sounded annoyed at this early morning intrusion.

'I hope I didn't wake you, Mr Campbell,' Lynne said. 'But I have to—'

'You didn't wake me,' Campbell broke in, slightly brusque. 'You caught us on the point of leaving for our country house. We were supposed to leave last night. What's the emergency you mentioned to my wife?'

Her voice unsteady Lynne told him what had happened with Bill.

'Mrs Travers, you can't expect the police to go after your ex-husband on the strength of what you've just told me,' Campbell said in dismissal. 'Do you know how many family squabbles occur every day in a city the size of New York? The police don't have the manpower to cope with them!'

'This is not a family squabble!' How could he be so insensitive? 'My ex-husband is threatening to maim my little girl. It's obvious in what he's said!'

'From what you've told me, Mr Travers is a nasty individual. He's behaving in a manner we could expect.'

'Then why did you insist I should not fight the visitation rights?' Lynne was too distraught to be diplomatic.

'Because we had no way of stopping it,' Campbell told her. 'To all outward appearances your ex-husband is an intelligent man. A loving father. We couldn't possibly have persuaded Judge Erickson not to grant him visitation rights. And frankly, Mrs Travers, I don't believe your husband means to carry out those vague threats.'

'Bill has custody of Susie until 6 p.m. tomorrow night.' Lynne tried to thrust ugly images from her mind. 'I'm terrified of what he may do to her. I must get her back. Mr Campbell, tell us what to do. We'll try anything.'

'I'm sorry. My wife and I have to leave now. We have a long, hot drive ahead of us.' He paused in contemplation. Lynne waited expectantly. 'You might consider talking to Judge Erickson. Though I doubt that—'

'Would you know where we can reach her?' Lynne pounced. On a Saturday morning in July, she could be anywhere.

'I don't know where the Judge lives. I'm sure you can track that down. But I'm convinced you're unduly concerned. Travers is not a psychotic. He holds down a responsible position. He has no record of violence—other than what you've told me.' Campbell's voice was guarded. It seemed to Lynne that he was questioning her reliability. Then she heard his wife calling to him. 'You'll have to excuse me,' he said with a note of finality and hung up.

'Did he give you an address?' Ira asked while Lynne put down the receiver.

'No. He just suggested we contact Judge Erickson.' Defeat closed in around Lynne. 'He doesn't know where she lives.'

'Let's see if she has a listed phone number.' Ira was sombre. This hardly seemed likely. 'Where's the Manhattan directory?'

Lynne and Ira searched the Manhattan phone directory. In desperation they tried information in random communities in Westchester County and Connecticut. Lynne was exasperated by their lack of success.

'We have to locate Judge Erickson.' Lynne clung to the possibility that Judge Erickson would help them. 'We must know somebody who'll have a lead to her.' And suddenly a name leapt into her mind. 'Jessica Meyers!' Ira had met Jessica, one of Lynne's special friends. It was Jessica, moved on now to better things, who had brought Lynne to Marty and Nationwide Publications. 'Jessica ran several wine and cheese parties before the last election. She campaigns like mad for any competent woman running for political office.' Lynne darted to the phone in a surge of confidence. 'Jessica will have a contact that can put us in touch with Judge Erickson.'

'It's early to be phoning on Saturday morning—' Ira was uneasy about this move.

'Jessica will understand.' Lynne was confident. She concentrated on dialling for a moment. Jessica had never met Bill, but she would be sympathetic and helpful. 'She has two kids. She'll know how I feel.'

Jessica's husband, Melvin, answered the phone. He reported that she was not at home. She was out on an early morning walking tour of Lower Manhattan. He expected her back about noon.

'Call Jessica a little past twelve,' he told Lynne. 'But if you can't make it until later, she'll be here. She'll be working at home the rest of the day. She's got to finish some freelance copy-editing assignment.'

At Lynne's behest Melvin went to search for Judge Erickson's address. A few minutes later he confessed he was unable to locate it.

'Jessica has a filing system nobody else can interpret,' he explained ruefully. 'Call later. If she doesn't have it, she'll know somebody who'll give it to her.'

Gently, Ira pointed out that it was useless to leave for the zoo before 9.30. Because to be idle was to dwell on the fears that shredded her composure, Lynne forced herself into routine activities. With Ira's help she made up the bed. Telling herself that Ira was right; nothing would happen to Susie. She was overreacting. Yet her throat was tight with alarm.

She washed the dishes by hand rather than stacking them in the dishwasher. She laundered the pretty, white dotted Swiss dress Susie had worn to a birthday party early in the week. She must keep busy.

'Bill will take Susie to the zoo in the morning,' Lynne predicted. 'He'll watch baseball on TV in the afternoon.' But *where* would he watch the baseball game?

'Scout for some snapshots of Susie,' Ira instructed. 'We'll show them around at the zoo.' They both realised that the trip to the zoo offered only meagre hope, yet they clutched at the possibility that Bill would take Susie there. Making this effort masked their sense of hammering at a stone wall.

At 9.30 a.m. Lynne and Ira left the apartment. By 10 a.m. they were walking down the two flights of stairs that led into the park at Fifth Avenue and Sixty-Fourth Street. They turned to the right, walked past the ivy garbed, dark-brick structure with the air of a medieval fortress. The hands of the zoo clock indicated the time as 10.04. They followed a couple with a toddler to the admission booth, where they joined the line. A few minutes later Ira handed over a five dollar bill for their admission.

Several vendors were already set up for business. Colourful balloons and inflated images of Barney the Clown floated above a selling cart. Ice cream and Italian ices were enticing early arrivals in the morning heat. Lynne pulled a sheaf of colour snapshots from her shoulder bag.

'Excuse me—' On impulse she approached

the balloon seller. 'Have you seen this little girl this morning?'

'We just opened, lady,' he reproached good-humouredly. But he obliged with a keen scrutiny. 'No, I ain't seen her. A kid as cute as that I'd remember.'

'Thank you.' Lynne returned the snapshots to her purse. How many others had come to the zoo to look for a missing child?

'Honey, they couldn't be here yet,' Ira pointed out. 'We came in with the first arrivals.'

'I'm not thinking straight,' Lynne conceded. How could she think straight in the midst of a nightmare?

Wrapped in unreality—remembering how Susie adored the seals—Lynne led Ira to the huge, rock-centred pool where the seals cavorted, carrying on exuberant flirtations with the watchers. *How could Susie be hurt here?*

Her eyes skimming every face about them, Lynne walked on impulse to the nearby ice cream cart. She showed the snapshots to the vendor. Her eyes clung to his face while he squinted at each snapshot in turn. He shook his head.

'Pretty kid.' His eyes were curious,

but an approaching customer aborted questions.

'Let's go this way.' Ira slid an arm about her waist. A young woman with a child about Susie's age smiled at them. The young woman thought Ira and she were lovers, Lynne guessed—spending a beautiful morning at the zoo. How could she know the terror that had brought them here?

Clinging to Ira's hand, Lynne led him to the next section. Here behind a tall, glass enclosure and with a moat-like separation of crystal water providing additional privacy the monkeys clamoured about the towering grey rocks in high spirits. Lynne searched the young faces that hovered along the walk—all radiating jubilant spirits. Susie wasn't here.

'Let's go back and sit on one of the benches near the entrance,' Ira said. 'If they come in, we can't miss them.'

Walking with a renewed sense of purpose, they went to the entrance and sat on a bench where they would see every new arrival. Now Ira focused on a vendor of soft drinks. He headed—perspiring in yet another day of record-breaking heat—to the purveyor of cold liquid refreshment.

Lynne scanned the faces of the hordes of children that approached. Her anxiety was accelerating. This was a wild goose chase, her mind jeered. She had *assumed* Bill would bring Susie here—because she wanted to believe it.

Ira returned with plastic cups of ice-islanded soft drinks and handed one to Lynne with an encouraging smile.

'I can't remember where the polar bears are,' Lynne fretted, feeling sick as she remembered Bill's voice on the phone: *Susie's still pretty. She would have grown up to look just like you. She wouldn't be pretty with an arm chewed off, would she?* No! Bill was just trying to frighten her.

'We'll find them in a few minutes,' Ira promised. 'It's the logical place for him to bring her.'

'She adores the polar bears,' Lynne said plaintively, 'but I just don't remember where they are. I've been here often enough with Susie—I should know.' It was weird to be at the zoo without Susie.

'Let's finish our drinks and go look for the bears.' Ira was struggling to seem casual, but Lynne sensed he shared her frustration.

They drained their cups. Ira dumped

112

them in a nearby receptacle. He inquired about the locale of the bears, and they pushed their way through the swelling crowd in the indicated direction.

One huge white bear splashed in the water with obvious pleasure. Another lay supine on a rock, dozing in the sun. This weather was rough on furred animals. Lynne sympathised.

All at once she was assaulted by a vision of Bill—pretending to be the indulgent but reckless father—scaling the tall, glass enclosure to straddle the top with Susie in tow—forbidden though it was. The awkward position would be precarious. A cry would go up from the onlookers as Susie fell from Bill's grasp. A mammoth paw could dart out to grab Susie's small, slender arm. A mouth could chew at that arm before anyone could intervene.

With a stifled moan Lynne swung away from the glass enclosure. She fought against a wave of sickness.

'Lynne?' Ira was solicitous.

'I'm all right,' she managed. How could she be all right when she didn't know what madness Bill was fomenting? 'But I can't stay here—'

Again, they roamed about the paths

of the zoo. Silent, their eyes searching among the children who darted with the swift, agile grace of the young—oblivious of the heat.

Lynne consulted her watch. The morning was disappearing. Every hour—every minute—counted. Why had she been so sure Bill would bring Susie here? She was clutching at any feeble hope. Why couldn't the police put their machinery into operation—before something awful happened?

They were no closer to finding Susie than they had been twelve hours ago. *Was she still all right? Were they already too late?*

Chapter Ten

Bill finished the final lap of his jogging along the Saturday-morning-busy stretch of concrete that lined the Hudson River in the West Seventies. The late morning sun bathed the cabin cruisers at the boat basin on his left in dazzling gold and helped to mask the greyness of the water.

He wasn't out of breath. Six months ago he would have been panting by this point. He was in great shape again. As good as he was in college.

Slowed down to a walk, he headed up the curving, foliage-flanked path that led up to Riverside Drive. He was aware of the admiring glances of a pair of girls stretched out on the grass in shorts and too-small T-shirts. Subconsciously he adopted a macho swagger. Knowing that he was an object of lust in running shorts and an Adolfo shirt.

He could have been at the top of the sports heap if he'd trained—except that his temper would always get in the way. How many people in this world had his spatial skills? When he played golf with Jim, he had him strung out with excitement. He'd hit the ball so it missed the hole by a quarter-inch, letting the old boy win with a real thrill. As a pitcher he could put the ball any place he liked. But you had to put up with too much shit in the sports world.

He was glad one of the shrinks had shoved him into jogging. Most of the time those sons-of-bitches didn't know what the hell they were doing. All that shit about his not being honest with them. Bill grinned. He was never honest with any shrink. You told them what you felt like telling them.

He hadn't gone to Weinstein—the last shrink—in three months. He didn't want to talk about his adolescence. Why did they always try to dredge up everything you were trying to forget?

A young couple with a little girl who looked strikingly like Susie—before he cut her hair—was strolling towards him. Lynne would be mad as hell if she knew he'd left Susie alone in the apartment. So what? She was asleep.

A rather pretty young woman in advanced pregnancy, walking between two men, cast a covert glance in his direction. Ready to try for another right now, he guessed. Whose kid was she carrying? Her husband's or some guy she'd picked up for a night?

God, Lynne had put up a show when she was pregnant. Like this was the greatest event of her life. Pretending all the time the baby was his. Carrying on about how they'd be a real family now.

She came back to him all blown up already, only he was too stupid to catch on. Pulling that preemie bit. She was plain lucky that Susie weighed in under five pounds. That was the only reason she could pull it off. And that bastard doctor, backing her all the way.

At Riverside Drive Bill paused, conscious of hunger. Sharon kept nothing but beer and orange juice in her refrigerator. He'd made himself two cups of black instant coffee before he came out to jog. Now he was ready for breakfast.

He'd walk up to Zabar's and bring back breakfast, he decided. Closing his mind to the unavoidable confrontation with Jim Sexton. Zabar's would be a madhouse on Saturday morning, but it was an 'in' place. He'd enjoy pushing through the crowd to buy bagels with cream cheese and Nova.

For a little while last night, soothed by the beers, he had fantasised about pretending to go to Dallas with Lynne and the kid. If he picked up some chick and took her down there, who in Dallas would know it wasn't his wife? He'd have no trouble shacking up with somebody who could play the scene. But before they left for Dallas, Jim meant to have Lynne and him out to the Ridgefield house. That killed it.

He went to Zabar's, shopped, and returned to the apartment. He checked his watch as he entered the lobby. It was almost 11.30. Susie ought to be awake by now.

He heard the sound of the TV while he fished for the keys. A Saturday morning cartoon was on the tube. Susie was awake. He unlocked the door and walked inside.

'Daddy?' Susie sounded scared. Did she think he'd gone off and left her here? 'Daddy?' She uncurled herself from her position before the television set and rose to her feet. Still in her nightie and clutching the smallest of the cats.

'I went out to get some breakfast for us,' he alibied, holding up the brown bag from Zabar's. 'Bagels and cream cheese and Nova. Go and get us two glasses of orange juice to drink with it.'

'I didn't know where you were.' Soft reproach in her voice. Just like a woman. Looking at her was like looking at Lynne. He was beginning to feel rotten again.

'I thought you'd be asleep.' He crossed to collapse into a chair. He could jog four miles and not be winded, but in this heat his muscles felt the workout. He'd have to shower before they cut out of here. He was sweating like a pig. Satisfaction washed over him for a moment. Lynne must be sweating, too. But not from the heat. 'Susie, go get the juice,' he repeated. 'After we eat, I'll shower. Then we'll decide what we want to do today.'

The smallest Siamese came brushing up against his leg while the other leapt up onto the sofa. The little one reminded him of the kitten they had the first year they were married. Lynne cried when it got killed. She never knew he'd run it down with the car. It had been so easy. After that he didn't have to bother about a dumb cat around the house.

Susie came back with two glasses of orange juice and sat cross-legged on the floor to eat her bagel.

'Daddy, you said we'd go to the zoo today.'

'Too hot,' Bill dismissed in distaste.

'Daddy, you promised,' Susie accused.

'I told you, it's too hot,' Bill snapped. All of a sudden he wanted to get out of the apartment. it was closing in on him. They'd get in the car and go somewhere. He had a lot to do this weekend. Time to think about how to do it. 'Susie, we'll find a place that sells frozen yoghurt,' he soothed. 'You'd like that, wouldn't you?'

Susie nodded enthusiastically.

'Daddy, where's the Mama cat? I couldn't find her anywhere.'

'There's no Mama cat,' Bill said. 'Just these two here.'

Susie frowned.

'There were three cats last night. I remember. The Mama cat, the Papa cat and the baby cat.'

'Two cats.' Christ, why didn't she shut up? All he needed now was a nagging kid.

'Maybe Mommie and Ira will take me to the zoo next week.' Susie moved away from the problem of the missing cat. *Ira again.* 'I'll ask Mommie.' Susie was pleased with this possibility. 'But there were three cats last night,' she picked up again. 'I saw them.'

Bill pulled himself to his feet. He didn't want to think about that bitchy cat. Nor about that other cat, that rotten summer when he was fifteen. Nothing would have happened if the cat hadn't brushed up against him that way.

'I'm going to shower.' Lynne and Ira were having themselves a ball while he got stuck with the kid. All Lynne ever thought about was herself. She didn't care what she did to him. But he knew how to get back at her. His mind was suddenly a mix-master, churning images of Lynne. Lynne with her eyes red and swollen from crying. Lynne screaming hysterically. Wishing she was dead. Lynne suffering the way she was making him suffer. 'When I'm out of the shower, we're going out.'

'Where to?' Susie seemed ambivalent about this.

'For a long drive.' Exhilaration surged through him. *He knew where they were going.* He could do it out there with no sweat. Nobody would ever know. 'We're getting out of this stinking, hot city.'

It was time to stop stalling. He knew how to pay Lynne off for cheating him out of Dallas. She'd pay, oh yes, she'd pay.

Chapter Eleven

'Ira, there's no sense in our just sitting here,' Lynne said. The wave of sickness that had attacked her at the sight of the bears had subsided. They had no time for such nonsense.

Ira squinted at his watch.

121

'We should phone Jessica in a few minutes. You're sure you feel all right?' His face was solicitous.

'I'm all right,' she said. 'Let's go.'

They left the bench and headed for the entrance.

'Lynne, give me those snapshots of Susie,' Ira said in sudden resolve, pausing a few feet from a line-up of vendors. 'You won't be upset if you don't get them back?'

'No. I have the negatives—' She tried to read his mind.

'This is another wild goose chase,' he warned.

'That doesn't matter.' They must try anything that had one crumb of hope of leading them to Susie. She reached into her purse and brought out the snapshots.

'Write Jessica's phone number on the back of each,' Ira told her, and Lynne hastily fumbled in her shoulder bag for a pen. 'Her husband said she'd be home the rest of the day, didn't he?'

'That's right.'

Lynne stood at one side while Ira conferred with a series of vendors. His pitch was the same to each. A phone call leading them to Susie would earn the caller a hundred dollars. Jessica Meyers would take messages. He would be in constant contact with her. A call would bring him right back to the zoo.

Lynne and Ira left the zoo to search for a public phone. Jessica wasted no time tracking down Judge Erickson's address and phone number when Lynne briefed her on the urgency of the situation.

'I'll stand by for calls.' Jessica was eager to be helpful. 'If a call comes in, Melvin will shoot right over to the zoo to check with the vendor and then trail Susie until you get there.' She hesitated. 'Lynne, I don't know if Judge Erickson is in town on a hot Saturday afternoon.'

'We'll have to try.' Lynne refused to consider failure. 'If Judge Erickson would give us some kind of warrant, then the police will have to start looking.'

'Don't phone,' Jessica advised. 'Go to the apartment. Make sure to use Bessie Bartlett's name. Bessie's been trying cases before Judge Erickson for fifteen years. Tell her Bessie sent you over. Bessie will confirm if Erickson checks with her.'

Judge Erickson lived in a substantial, old building on Park Avenue in the Seventies. The lobby exuded an air of prosperity and conservatism. The doorman at first rejected Ira's request that he should call up to the Judge's apartment to ask if she would see them.

'Judge Erickson leaves word when she's expecting people,' he said. Ira's hand emerged from the pocket of his slacks. Greenery performed the anticipated reversal. 'Well, if it's important, I can ask her,' the doorman conceded.

'Tell Judge Erickson a friend of Bessie Bartlett must speak with her for five minutes.' Ira grasped at Jessica's directive.

Lynne and Ira waited while the doorman conferred with someone other than the Judge. Then the Judge herself was at the intercom.

'Rudolph, ask the caller why Miss Bartlett hasn't phoned me herself,' they heard the Judge say. 'I resent this kind of intrusion unless I know it's legitimate.'

Ira reached for the phone and took it from Rudolph's hand before he could object.

'Judge Erickson, please forgive us.' Ira's voice was restrained, yet it commanded attention. 'The life of a little girl is in your hands. The child of divorced parents whose case you heard.'

Judge Erickson hesitated for a split-second.

'Five minutes,' she stipulated. 'Apartment 12–A.'

Lynne and Ira hurried into the small but elegant lobby and waited before the bank of elevators. After what seemed an interminable wait, an elevator hissed to a stop. The door slid open. Lynne darted inside. Ira was seconds behind her. *Let Judge Erickson give them a writ. Something they could run to the police with.*

Lynne looked at her watch. It was 12.38 p.m. She had not seen Susie for over eighteen hours. Was she all right? If Bill hurt that sweet baby, she'd kill him. She wouldn't let him live.

'Tell the Judge about Bill's psychiatric treatment,' Ira said while they emerged from the elevator.

'Five psychiatrists in less then two years,' Lynne recalled. 'He was always running.'

'Of course, psychiatric records are confidential,' Ira said soberly, 'but if Judge Erickson talks to the last one and explains the situation, he might feel a moral obligation to help.'

'The last one was Dr Everett Weinstein. I don't know if Bill's still seeing him.

125

He hasn't mentioned Dr Weinstein for months.'

The elevator stopped. Lynne's throat went dry. Ira and she rushed from the elevator to Judge Erickson's apartment door. The hall was lushly carpeted; the wallpaper attractive. Only two apartments on each floor.

Ira rang the doorbell. They heard the chimes echoing inside. A maid admitted them and asked that they follow her to the library. Through a wall of glass in the living room on their right Lynne saw a large oval table set for six on the landscaped terrace.

Judge Erickson sat behind a desk in the library, rich with bookcases that reached from floor to ceiling. The oak panelling of the room was an effective contrast for her prematurely white hair and tanned skin.

'We'll have to make this brief,' Judge Erickson told them. 'My husband and I are expecting luncheon guests.' She leaned forward, elbows on the desk. Attentive.

Lynne realised Ira wanted her to do the talking. He suspected a mother's plea would be more eloquent than his. She tried to be spare in words.

'Mrs Travers,' Judge Erickson interrupted

with strained patience after a few minutes, 'your ex-husband gave your daughter a haircut? That's hardly a threat against her life.'

'Scissors in Bill's hands were a threat,' Lynne insisted, 'when he hinted at maiming her. He called at six in the morning to talk about a little girl whose arm was chewed off by a bear—' Lynne's voice choked up.

Judge Erickson could not completely suppress an exclamation of annoyance.

'When you called upstairs, you said a child's life was at stake. This is a domestic difference between your former husband and yourself!'

'Judge Erickson, Bill's a violent man. Not the man who appeared so intelligent and charming in your courtroom.'

'Mrs Travers, I don't remember either your husband or you in my courtroom,' Judge Erickson said bluntly. 'With the number of cases I have to hear each week, the faces become blurs. But the situation is familiar. Any number of times in the course of a year a former husband decides to fight with his ex-wife.' Her eyes moved to Ira. 'Particularly when the wife has acquired other romantic attachments.'

'Do those husbands threaten to maim their daughters?' Lynne challenged.

Judge Erickson frowned. Her eyes swung past Lynne to the door. Only now did Lynne realise the maid stood there.

'My luncheon guests have arrived.' Judge Erickson rose to her feet in dismissal. 'I'm sure Mr Travers will return your daughter safely tomorrow evening.'

'Judge Erickson, this man has a history of psychiatric treatment,' Ira said with unwary desperation. 'If you talk to his psychiatrist and—'

'I will not invade Mr Travers' privacy.' Judge Erickson's voice was a staccato reproof, her gaze scathing. 'Do you know the statistics on the prevalence of psychiatric treatment in today's troubled world? One in ten? One in eight? Mrs Travers, I suggest you go for counselling. Learn how to handle yourself in domestic crises. They don't belong in a judge's chambers. Lila,' she spoke to the maid, 'please show these people to the door.'

Chapter Twelve

Lynne and Ira walked out into the humid day. She was dizzy with disappointment. She had convinced herself that Judge Erickson would make it possible to bring in the police.

In a city of eight million—or whatever the current population of New York was supposed to be—how could they expect to find Bill and Susie without the police machinery in action? Every time she looked at a clock, she was filled with fresh terror. Clocks were ticking away the hours, the minutes of Susie's life. Teams of detectives ought to be combing the city for her this minute.

'Ira, nobody believes me!' Lynne burst out as they walked without direction for a few yards. 'They didn't hear Bill on the telephone! They don't know him!' She had never come face to face with such a feeling of helplessness. Even in her worst moments with Bill, logic had come to her rescue. But logic was a dead-end street now. 'Ira, how are we going to find Susie?' she cried out in desperation.

Ira prodded her towards an unoccupied public telephone.

'Call Jessica,' he said with manufactured calm. 'See if she's heard from anybody.' But Lynne knew his anxiety was right on the heels of her own.

She moved to the phone, fumbling in her purse for change.

'Let me try Bill again before I call Jessica.'

Ira pulled change from his pocket and handed it to her. She dropped coins into the slot. Maybe Ira was right when he said Bill was just trying to scare her. Bill's black sense of humour had unnerved her before. Maybe Bill and Susie were back at the apartment now.

She dialled, grateful for Ira's protective presence. She heard the ring at the other end. *Answer. Please God, make Bill answer.* Her hand ached from the tightness with which she gripped the phone. Over and over a monotonous ring echoed from the other end of the line.

'Lynne, they're not there.' Ira's voice was compassionate but firm. 'Hang up. Dial Jessica.'

Lynne cut the connection, dropped the returned quarter in the slot again and waited for a dial tone. Now she dialled Jessica's number.

'Hello.' Jessica's voice was slightly breathless with anticipation. She was hoping this was a call from the zoo, Lynne realised.

'Jessica, it's Lynne—'

'What happened with Judge Erickson?'

'We struck out.' Lynne fought to hold on to her composure. 'Nobody called from the zoo?'

'Not so far. Come back to the apartment. Let's figure out our next move.'

'This is unreal.' Despair turned Lynne cold despite the record-breaking heat. 'I can't believe I let Bill walk out with Susie that way.'

'The court gave him visitation rights. You couldn't do otherwise. It's a normal situation that occurs every weekend to millions of mothers.' Jessica tried to sound optimistic. 'Probably Bill is just trying to make you sweat out this whole weekend.'

'And I remember Bill's rage. You don't know how important that promotion was to him. He was moving into top management. He blames me for putting it out of his reach.' Lynne was strangling in anguish.

'Jessica, I've got to find my baby!'

'Come up to the apartment with Ira.' Jessica was gentle. 'This is a team effort now.'

Lynne and Ira cabbed across the park to Jessica and Melvin's comfortable West Side apartment. Jessica had set out a festive array of cold cuts and bread. Melvin went out to the kitchen to bring in a pitcher of iced coffee.

'I know you're not in the mood for food.' Jessica read her mind. 'But you have to eat. On Saturday mornings Melvin raids Zebar's. We're sybaritic and lazy over the weekend. Today both kids are off to the beach with friends, so I don't have to feel guilty because I'm not leaning over a hot stove.'

Lynne allowed herself to be prodded into a chair at the table. How could she eat with Bill's voice ricocheting in her brain? How could he behave this way towards his own child?

'A hundred to one we're overreacting,' Ira said again as he seated himself beside Lynne and eyed the glistening strip of Nova nestled on the cream cheese-spread half of bagel Jessica had shifted to his plate. 'Still, let's try everything humanly possible to track down Susie and her father.'

'Why are the police so difficult?' Lynne railed. 'They have the means to find Susie!'

'They can't act,' Melvin said. 'No crime has been committed. No threat that fits within legal terminology.'

'You said Bill has been going to a shrink?' Jessica was contemplative.

'He was. I don't know that he's still going.'

'Do you know the shrink's name?'

'The most recent was a man named Weinstein. Dr Everett Weinstein.'

'Call him,' Jessica urged. 'Explain the situation. Maybe he knows something to bring to the attention of the police. Something that might spur them into action.'

Lynne gazed at Jessica in indecision.

'Honey, let's try to reach Dr Weinstein,' Ira joined in. 'Under the circumstances he might help.'

Dr Weinstein was listed in the Manhattan directory. With Ira beside her for moral support Lynne dialled his number. She frowned at the sound of the recorded voice that responded.

'Dr Weinstein is away from the city for

the weekend,' a feminine voice informed her. 'He will be back in his office at 10 a.m. on Monday morning. For emergency situations please phone Dr Ralph Galehouse at—' Without waiting for a phone number Lynne hung up. Then she was sorry she had not waited.

'He's away until Monday,' Lynne explained to the others. 'He has a doctor covering for him—' Should she have hung on for the covering doctor's number?

'A covering psychiatrist won't dig into the files and release information without Weinstein's permission,' Ira guessed.

'Call him,' Melvin urged. 'Maybe he knows some way to reach Dr Weinstein.'

Lynne called Weinstein's number again. This time she waited for the number of the covering psychiatrist. Dr Galehouse answered himself. Dr Weinstein could not be reached. He was away on a boat for the weekend. Dr Galehouse had no access to Dr Weinstein's files. He was apologetic but firm. The matter would have to wait until Dr Weinstein returned.

'All right, we have to come up with another approach,' Jessica conceded. But her eyes belied her air of optimism. Bill was so devious, Lynne thought exhaustedly.

How were they going to find him? Before he did something awful to Susie. *Had it already happened?*

'We can't rule out the zoo.' Melvin was trying to be hopeful. 'It's a long shot, but we have to keep this phone covered.'

'I'll try Bill's apartment again.' Maybe it was absurd, but she had to make the effort, Lynne told herself.

'Look, it's a wide area out there,' Melvin pushed ahead, 'so let's try to cut down the odds. Where would be the most logical place for Bill to go with Susie?'

'The weather is hot,' Ira picked up. 'Lynne says Bill loathes the heat.' At the phone Lynne waited for the familiar ring. Let it ring ten times, she ordered herself. Wasn't that what the phone company said to do? 'Bill may have taken Susie to the beach. Let's narrow it down further—' He waited until Lynne put the phone down. 'What beach does Bill like?'

'We took a cottage one summer at Fire Island. And he talked yesterday evening about missing this weekend at Fire Island,' Lynne recalled. A flicker of hope welled in her. 'Do you suppose he took Susie out there?' To which community? There were several.

'What exactly did he say about Fire Island?' Jessica probed.

'I'd just told him I'd never remarry him. And that—that I was seeing someone else.' Lynne struggled to reconstruct those heated moments. 'He was furious. He said—' She squinted in thought. 'He said, "I was supposed to go out to Fire Island. I gave up a gorgeous chick so Susie and I could have the weekend together."'

'He wouldn't take Susie out to a scene like that,' Ira said with conviction. 'If he was chasing after a girl, he wouldn't want to be seen in the father image. Macho, yes. Paternal, no.'

'What about the country?' Jessica asked. 'Would any of his friends have a country place? Or beach house?'

'Bill has no friends,' Lynne said flatly. 'He cultivates people who might be useful to him in business. If nothing develops fast, he drops them and looks elsewhere.' But she was searching her mind. 'It's not exactly country, but his boss lives up in Ridgefield, Connecticut. A house with two acres and a pool. Bill drives up to play golf with him some Saturday mornings.' Excitement deepened her voice. 'That's where he must have gone with Susie.

Up to Ridgefield. Show Jim Sexton his daughter. Stalling him.'

'Let's try to call this Sexton.' Ira grabbed at the lead. 'That could be the answer.'

Ira dialled for Ridgefield information, asked for Sexton's number. The operator reported no listing.

'Sexton's unlisted. That isn't unusual,' Ira admitted. 'Lynne, do you know anybody who might be able to give you his number? Somebody from Bill's office?'

'His secretary,' Lynne supplied. 'She might have it.' Bill's secretary was a sweet, plain woman in her thirties, supporting a small son and a husband who was more often unemployed than employed. 'Bonnie Lane.' Lynne fished the secretary's name from the recesses of her brain. It had touched her that a woman so aware of her plainness could be called Bonnie. But Bill had said she was the most efficient secretary in the organisation. 'She lives in Brooklyn Heights.' In a rent-controlled building that was her pride.

'We have a Brooklyn directory.' Melvin strode across the room and dug the directory from a pile-up of books. 'Let's hope she's listed.'

Melvin found a B. Lane on Hicks Street. Lynne was willing to check it out. But she couldn't just come out and ask Bonnie for Jim Sexton's phone number. While she searched her mind for a logical alibi, Ira broke out in a frenzied sneezing fit.

'It's that time of year,' Ira apologised.

'And Jessica has to have fifty-six plants hanging around the apartment,' Melvin chuckled.

She'd say that Bill took Susie off for the weekend, and she'd just discovered Susie went off without her allergy medication, Lynne plotted. Susie suffered from no allergies, but Bonnie wouldn't know that.

Lynne went to the phone and dialled. Her heart pounding. All at once Susie felt closer to her. *Let Bonnie be home. Let her know Jim Sexton's phone number. Let Susie and Bill be up in Ridgefield. Then this nightmare would be over.*

'Hello.' A feminine voice replied on the second ring.

'Bonnie?' Lynne's throat constricted with excitement.

'Yes.' Warm in greeting despite doubts as to Lynne's identity.

'Bonnie, this is Lynne Travers.' She had not taken back her maiden name. That

138

would be a barrier between Susie and her. 'I'm sorry to be disturbing you this way on a Saturday.'

'It's no problem,' Bonnie said blithely. 'Actually I'm glad somebody took me away from the typewriter. I'm doing some freelance typing over the weekend, and I welcome an interruption.'

'I suppose you know that Bill and I are divorced?'

Belatedly she realised that nobody at the office knew. If it had been kept a secret from Jim Sexton, Bill couldn't tell anyone at the office.

'No.' Her regret was genuine. 'I had no idea, Lynne.'

Bonnie sounded troubled. She lived in a world where the wife was a chattel to her husband.

'Bill has Susie for the weekend. I believe he went up to Ridgefield with her. I just this minute discovered I hadn't packed Susie's allergy medication. She only takes it when she has an attack, so she might not even need it. But I'd feel lots better if I could call Bill and let him know that there's a non-prescription drug he can give her in an emergency. I just can't seem to locate Jim Sexton's phone number. You

139

know, you file somebody's number away for safekeeping and then you can't find it—' She was breathless with the effort to sound casual.

'I can give it to you, Lynne.' Bonnie was eager to be helpful. 'Just hold on a minute.'

Bonnie came back with Sexton's phone number. Lynne apologised for her abruptness, reiterating her anxiety to reach Bill, and said goodbye. Now she dialled Jim Sexton's number. The phone rang for an unbelievably long time. She hung on, willing somebody to reply. It was a large house. Fourteen rooms, Bill said. It might take time to reach a phone.

Lynne looked at her watch as she waited. It was 1.48 p.m. Bill had walked out of the apartment with Susie almost twenty hours ago. His last call was almost eight hours ago.

'Hi.' A cheerful young male voice responded.

'Is this the Sexton residence?'

'That's right,' the voice said. Lynne heard a feminine giggle in the background.

'May I please speak to Mr Sexton?' Lynne asked.

'He's not here. He's playing golf. Can

140

I give him a message?' This would be Jim Sexton's seventeen-year-old son. The youngest of the four Sexton children. Alone in the house with a girlfriend, Lynne surmised, and impatient to be off the phone.

'Do you know when he'll be back?' Lynne persisted.

'No. My mother's away, too, so I can't ask her.' He was trained to be polite, but this was a drag.

'Could you tell me where he plays golf?' Could they have Jim Sexton paged? Was Bill with him? *Where was Susie?*

'I'm not sure where he's playing.' The son was guarded. He'd been trained, also, not to give out information. 'Would you like to leave your name?'

'Would you know if Bill Travers is with him?' Frustration tied knots in Lynne's stomach.

'I don't know who he's playing with. Can I give him a message?' The tone of his voice clearly said, buzz off.

'Thank you, no.' Lynne put down the phone.

'No information on Sexton except that he's at the golf course,' Ira summed up, his face serious.

'He's at a golf course,' Lynne confirmed. 'His son didn't know which one. Or refused to say. How many golf courses can there be near Ridgefield?' Hope seeped through. 'Can't we try them all? Bill just might be with him.'

'They won't page him on the course,' Ira pointed out. 'We can't reach him that way. We'll drive up,' Ira decided.

'To Ridgefield?' Melvin was sceptical.

'What about the zoo?' Jessica was uneasy. 'Suppose one of the vendors calls?'

'We can forget about the zoo,' Lynne conceded. 'If Bill was taking Susie to the zoo, he would have made it a morning trip. On a Saturday afternoon in town Bill would be in front of a TV watching baseball. Nobody could drag him to the zoo.'

'But he might drive up to play golf with his boss,' Ira picked up. 'We can be up there in just over an hour. We'd waste that much time trying to locate the golf courses and asking if Sexton was hanging around the clubhouse. It'll take us ten minutes to go to the garage to pick up my car. We can—'

'Take mine and save ten minutes,' Melvin interrupted and reached into a pocket for his keys. 'It's the '91 Dodge Spirit parked right in front of the building. Dark green.'

'Phone us when you come up with something,' Jessica called after them. 'We'll stand by here.'

Chapter Thirteen

In Melvin's Dodge Spirit Lynne and Ira sped up the Henry Hudson and into the Sawmill River Parkway. Traffic was miraculously light. Lynne checked with her watch at impatient intervals. Every minute was precious.

'We turn off at Katonah.' Ira fished directions from his memory. 'Take route 35 across country.' Normally a cautious driver, today he drove with a heavy foot on the gas pedal. Telegraphing his own alarm.

Lynne watched for police cars. They mustn't waste time stopping to collect a speeding ticket. How could she tell a traffic cop they were racing to save her baby's life? He wouldn't believe her.

In record-breaking time they left the Sawmill and raced across country into the attractive, affluent suburban community of Ridgefield, Connecticut. Ira located a gas station, enquired about the locale of golf courses in the area. Lynne scribbled down directions, pencil clutched between tense fingers.

'We'll try this one.' Ira indicated a name on the list. 'It's the nearest.'

They drove past rows of charming colonial houses set on meticulously cared-for lawns, past contemporary houses with vast expanses of glass. Watching for signs that would indicate they were approaching the golf course.

Lynne leaned forward at the sight of an uninterrupted stretch of green on their right. She spied a golf cart.

'It's along here.'

Her eyes strained for the view of a little girl with freshly cropped dark hair. But she saw no little girl. Bill and Susie could be somewhere else on the course. *Was Susie with him? Had he left her with a sitter?* She would behave if he took her along. She'd adore riding along with Bill and Jim Sexton on a golf cart.

'There's the clubhouse.' Ira nodded

ahead of them towards a bend in the road. A low, sprawling, white-brick structure sat behind tall, black, wrought-iron gates.

Lynne waited while Ira left the car to confer with a guard stationed in a booth at the entrance. She saw the guard reach for a telephone, talk briefly, then swing the gates wide. Ira returned to the car and slid behind the wheel.

'Sexton is a member here. We'll have to check at the desk to see if he's out on the course.'

Lynne sought to restrain her excitement. Bill must have rushed up here to talk to Sexton. He'd been livid at the thought of losing this promotion. He was so positive he was on the road to the top now. Bill had to be up here with Sexton.

Lynne and Ira walked into the starkly modern lobby. To the left was a dining room, its entrance screened by tall, green plants. They walked to the counter that faced the doorway. The man on duty checked the roster and informed them that Sexton had, indeed, played golf earlier. But now he was in the dining room having lunch.

'With a man and a little girl?' Lynne's eyes pleaded for confirmation.

'I didn't see Mr Sexton come in from the course,' the man explained. 'I was on my lunch hour.'

'We have an important message for Mr Sexton,' Ira explained. 'Could you please have him paged?'

'I'll have someone convey that to him at his table if you'll please give me your name.' The man was wary. 'We don't disturb our members in the dining room or on the course unless it's urgent. They come here to relax,' he added in reproof.

'Please tell Mr Sexton that we must talk to him about Bill Travers.' Ira made a show of confidence. 'Mr Sexton will understand.'

'But if you don't wish to give your name—' The man appeared affronted.

'Mr Sexton doesn't know me.' Ira was polite but firm. 'He knows Mr Travers. It's an urgent matter.'

'I wouldn't want to disturb Mr Sexton at luncheon without reason.' The man seemed ambivalent, but he was ringing a bell on the counter.

A note was sent to Sexton's table. He'd be annoyed at being disturbed, Lynne surmised. But that didn't matter. They couldn't ask for Bill. They had to ask for

146

Jim Sexton. If Bill wasn't there, they had to question Sexton about where he might be. But she didn't want to think that Bill was not sitting in the dining room. With Susie.

Within a few minutes Jim Sexton walked into the lobby. He crossed directly to the counter. The man on duty murmured to him and pointed towards Lynne and Ira. Sexton approached Lynne with an air of astonishment.

'How nice to see you, Lynne.' He extended a hand in greeting. His eyes grazed Ira as though distrustful of the presence of another man at Lynne's side. 'Has something happened to Bill?' Now he was solicitous.

'We're trying to contact him,' Ira explained because Lynne's throat was suddenly too tight for speech. 'Bill has their little girl with him. Susie's allergy medication was not packed in her valise. We brought it up to them.' Ira was covering for Bill. He didn't deserve it. 'This time of year is bad for allergy sufferers.' Ira was having allergy problems, Lynne realised. His eyes were watering. His nasal passages were clearly clogged.

'Bill isn't here.' Sexton was abrupt.

He was making conjectures about her relationship to Ira. He didn't know about the divorce.

'We—I thought Bill might have come up here with Susie.' Lynne fought to keep her voice even. 'He said they were driving up to Connecticut.'

'You didn't bother to ask where they would be staying?' Sexton was contemptuous of such an oversight. He was affronted by her appearance here with Ira. 'They're not here. If you'll excuse me, I'll return to my lunch.'

'Mr Sexton, would you have any idea where Bill might have gone?' Lynne trembled with disappointment. She had been so sure they'd be here.

'I have no idea where Bill has gone for the weekend,' Sexton said coldly. 'Please excuse me.' He headed back for the dining room.

Lynne and Ira returned to the car. This had been yet another futile effort. More wasted time. *Is it too late already? No, I won't believe that!*

'Ira, do you think he knows where Bill and Susie are?' Lynne asked as they drove away from the clubhouse.

'I doubt it,' Ira consoled.

'If he did, he wouldn't tell us.'

'Honey, would you mind if we stop somewhere for a cold drink?' Ira was apologetic. 'I think I'd better take my allergy medication. I've never learned to swallow pills dry.'

'Of course we'll stop.' She was contrite that she had ignored his obvious discomfort.

They found a Friendly's and went inside.

'We won't waste more than five minutes,' Ira promised. Two patrons had just vacated seats, which they took over.

Lynne and Ira communicated their need for fast service to the good-natured waitress on duty at their section. Two glasses of orange juice were whisked before them. Ira gulped down his pill and abandoned the remainder of the juice.

'Let's go, Lynne.' He reached for the check with one hand and fumbled for money with the other.

Lynne battled against panic as they drove back in the direction of the parkway. Where should they look now?

'Ira, let me try Bill's apartment again,' she said after a while. 'Just in case they've come back—'

'We'll find a phone at the Katonah

station. Try calling from there.' Ira was placating her. He didn't expect Bill to be at the apartment.

'All right, I'll call from Katonah.' Then her mind dwelt on the name of the suburban town. Why did she know it? Excitement propelled her to the edge of her seat as comprehension jogged into position. 'Ira, I just remembered. Dan Watkins lives in Katonah!' At least, he lived there two Christmases ago, when Bill and she had received a card from him.

'Who's Dan Watkins?' Ira reacted to her excitement.

'Bill's old college buddy. The only lasting friend I ever knew him to have. Dan was a witness at our wedding.' Recall was a shroud that threatened, for a moment, to suffocate her. 'We didn't see much of him after college. He went on to law school in Boston, and Bill and I came to New York. Dan joined a law firm in White Plains when he earned his degree. I've had the feeling that Bill sees him occasionally.'

'You think Bill might have come up here for the weekend?'

'He might have. Ira, let's try to find Dan.' *Let him still live in Katonah.*

'We'll check the Katonah phone directory,' Ira agreed. 'How recently do you think he may have seen Bill?'

'I don't know,' she acknowledged. There was so much she didn't know about Bill. 'But they were close at college. I remember Bill went away with Dan for the Thanksgiving weekend in our senior year. If he went to visit anybody, Ira, it would be Dan!'

Lynne vibrated with fresh hope.

Chapter Fourteen

Traffic on the expressway was congested. Cars moved for a hundred yards, then sat overheating for five minutes before proceeding for the next hundred yards. At this rate it would take them seven hours to get to the house, Bill seethed. If they didn't start moving, he'd have to cut off the air conditioning or the car would stall.

'Daddy, why wouldn't you let me phone Mommie?' Susie asked, tears threatening. The diversion of frozen yogurt was gone.

'I told you.' Why couldn't she be quiet?

'Your mother called and told me she was going to the beach. You were sleeping. She said not to wake you.'

'I wish you'd waked me.' Susie's face was forlorn. Poignantly stained by tears and chocolate yogurt. 'I wanted to talk to her.'

'You'll talk to her tomorrow night.'

Christ, Susie was going to be a pain in the ass. He was getting that rotten feeling again. He needed a clear head. He had to be sure he did everything right. Damn, he should have taken the pills with him.

He had never taken anybody out to the beach house except Dan. Twice during the college years, and then once after Lynne walked out on him. Lynne never knew about the house, he remembered in vicious satisfaction.

Wouldn't she be surprised! She loved walking along an empty stretch of beach.

The house was a shack. In the worse possible neighbourhood. His big inheritance from his grandmother, he jeered. He ought to sell it instead of throwing away tax money every year. But he knew he wouldn't sell it. It was where he went when he had to get his head together.

'When will we be there?' Susie asked

when the cars began to roll again.

'Soon.' His knuckles were white from the intensity with which he gripped the wheel. Why didn't she shut up? 'Take a nap.'

'Is the house on the beach?'

'We can bike there in a few minutes. Take a nap—'

'You've got a bike at the house?' Susie was impressed.

'An old one.'

'Daddy, when will we buy the doll you promised me?'

'When we get to Southampton.'

He could afford to fix up the house if he got the Dallas promotion. The address was great if nobody knew just where it was situated. *'My little place at Southampton.'* If there was a company plane, he could fly up from Dallas for some holiday weekends.

Thinking about redoing his grandmother's run-down summer place, he grew less tense. He visualised a sweeping expanse of glass. Another wing. A pool behind the house. Everything fenced in for privacy.

But he wouldn't get that vice-presidency. No fat bonuses. No stock options. Lynne had messed that up for him. When Sexton found out they were divorced, the old bastard would throw him out of the company. Lynne was doing this to him.

Again the traffic slowed to a crawl. He switched off the air conditioning. In five minutes the car would be like an oven. He rolled down the window on his side, leaned forward to roll down the window on the other side. Susie was asleep, her head propped against the door.

It would be so easy to shove open the door when the cars speeded up again. Right in front of an oncoming car. Excitement swarmed through him as he considered this. His hands were sweating. He had to handle this right. No mistakes.

Suppose something got into the newspapers? His folks might see it. He didn't trust them. They could make trouble for him. They didn't know they had a grandchild, but his name would be mentioned as the father.

Susie wasn't their grandchild. She just had their name. His name. He wished to hell she'd stop calling him 'Daddy'. He wasn't her father. He knew that when Lynne told him she was pregnant. He just hadn't wanted to face up to it until now. If his folks found out something had happened to Susie, they might get religious or something and decide to talk. He should have killed them long ago. They were the only ones who knew.

If his parents were dead, nobody would know what happened that rotten summer when he was fifteen.

They could have a fire in that old house up there, he plotted. Feeling a surge of pleasure as he visualised flames racing through the old farmhouse. Trapping those inside. He could take their supposed grandchild up there for a sentimental meeting.

He'd leave Susie with them while he went to shop for ice cream and cake to celebrate. He'd make sure the house burnt down while he was away. It was an old house. Built in 1837. Everybody knew those houses were tinderboxes.

No, he stopped himself. What the hell was the matter with him? If Susie died, Lynne would marry that son-of-a-bitch and have another kid. He wanted to sit back and watch Lynne suffer. If Susie was all messed up, she'd never marry again. She'd have to spend the rest of her life taking care of Susie. Feeling guilty.

Lynne didn't know his parents were alive. It pleased him that he had lied to her. When they were in college, he gave her a fancy story about being alone in the world. Women always lapped that up. To him his mother and father were dead.

They locked him up in that place—thirty-five kilometres out of Geneva—for three years. Washed him out of their lives. When he had got out—with a high school diploma—they had set him up in that stupid college on the West Coast. Mom and the old man wanted him as far away as they could manage. But he didn't stay, he remembered in triumph. He transferred to the school in Pennsylvania and then wrote them where to send the cheques. They didn't dare not send the money. They were scared of him.

The West Coast school didn't want a scandal. They let him transfer. That English lit. professor knew what was going to happen when she invited him to her apartment. So he lost his head and roughed her up! He didn't rape her like she claimed to the administration. The lady invited him.

Susie shifted in her sleep. She was hot and uncomfortable in the car. She'd be more uncomfortable before the weekend was over. He just had to work his way up to doing it. Figure out the best way. With no problems afterwards.

He'd make Lynne wish she was dead. She'd hurt for a long time. And he'd sit back and laugh.

Chapter Fifteen

Ira turned off the parkway and circled around the Katonah railroad station. Lynne's hand was on the door at her side before the car pulled to a full stop.

'There's a phone right on the platform,' Ira pointed, out but Lynne was already out of the car and hurrying in that direction.

Her hands were unsteady with excitement as she flipped through the pages of the slim Westchester County phone book. When she was about to concede defeat, the name jumped out at her. Daniel R. Watkins.

'He's here!' Lynne said as Ira arrived at her side.

'He may not be home,' Ira warned, knowing the hope that bloomed inside her.

Lynne dialled Dan's number, praying he

was home. Why hadn't she thought of Dan before?

'Hello.' A friendly, feminine voice responded.

'May I speak to Dan Watkins, please?' Was Dan married? How strange that they had received no word. Was this another Dan Watkins? Misgivings put a lid on hope.

'Who's calling, please?' Brisk and business-like.

'Lynne Travers. I knew Dan in college.' If this was the right Dan Watkins.

'Just a moment—'

The woman at the other end said nothing about Bill being there. But that didn't mean he wasn't.

'Watkins is home?' Ira asked.

Lynne nodded. Her throat tight with anticipation. She reached out for Ira's hand. Thank God for Ira. Let them get out of this awful mess intact, and she'd marry him instantly. Ira would be a wonderful father for Susie.

They had been grasping at any feeble lead. They needed a real direction. If Susie and Bill were not here—but no, she wouldn't let herself think that.

'Lynne!' Dan's voice was exuberant at

the other end. 'How good to hear from you! How's Bill? And Susie?'

Bill and Susie were not with Dan. This hope was demolished. But Dan was bright and perceptive. A lawyer. He'd help them.

'Bill and I are divorced—' She tried to gear herself for what must be said. 'Bill told you, didn't he?' He'd said something offhandedly, just after the divorce was granted, about running into Dan at the theatre.

'He didn't say a word about it!' Dan was astonished. 'How are you and Susie? I can't believe I've never seen her.'

'Dan, I'm frantic.' Lynne strained to hold on to her composure. 'Bill took Susie off for the weekend. A Family Court judge granted visitation rights. Dan—' Despite her determination her voice broke. 'He's been phoning me, making awful threats about what he's going to do to Susie. But I can't reach him. It's unreal. His own child! I've tried to talk to the police. They insist they can't take any action. They—'

'Where are you calling from?' Dan interrupted.

'The Katonah station.'

'Do you have a car?' Dan asked.

'Yes.'

'Drive over to the house. Let's talk about this.' Dan had always been the calm, steadying influence among their college clique, Lynne remembered.

'I'm with a friend,' she told Dan. 'Ira Edmonds.' She hesitated. 'We expect to be married soon.'

'The two of you drive right over to the house.' His voice softened. 'You'll meet my wife. We've been married almost two years.'

'I didn't know.' Now Lynne was astonished.

'I was surprised when you didn't answer when I wrote you about Andrea and me. I guess you never saw the letter.'

'No,' Lynne said. That must have been right after she left Bill.

'Let me give you directions,' Dan said with warmth. 'We're about three miles from the station.'

Lynne repeated the directions as Dan gave them to her. Ira scribbled them on the back of an envelope. She felt encouraged that they had made this contact. Yet worry crept into her mind that Bill might have called the apartment again. As long as he called, she knew Susie was unharmed. As

160

of that moment. But she had not heard from Bill since six o'clock that morning.

'Lynne, let's go.' Ira prodded her from the phone because she was frozen in fearful conjecture.

They drove along the winding roads to a weathered, shingled, colonial cape set on a fieldstone-flanked embankment, above a narrow brook. A charming, picture book house. Lynne read the name on the mailbox outside. Daniel and Andrea Watkins.

'This is it,' Lynne confirmed.

Ira turned into the uphill driveway and pulled to a stop. Eagerly Lynne thrust open the car door on her side, just as Dan emerged from the house.

'Lynne!' He charged forward in welcome, reaching out to draw her close. 'It's been too long.'

It was as though they were back at college, and Dan was consoling her after one of the battles she had with Bill. She always blamed herself; she was so afraid of losing Bill. She had closed her eyes to the violence in him that should have been apparent even then.

'Dan, this is Ira Edmonds,' she introduced. 'Dan was Bill's only real friend at college. Everyone liked Bill, but only Dan was close.'

'As close as anybody could get to Bill.' Dan's smile was enigmatic. 'Come inside and tell me what's happening.'

Dan's wife was a tall, slender blonde. Lynne liked her on sight. Andrea and Dan had met at law school. Both were with prestigious Westchester County law firms.

Over tall, frosty glasses of iced tea Lynne blurted out the horror of the past twenty-four hours. Andrea and Dan listened in sombre attention.

'In college everybody was drawn to Bill,' Dan told Andrea. 'He was good-looking and charismatic. He spoke French and German like a native and was a marvellous mimic. But I've never been entirely comfortable with Bill. He's unpredictable. To a lot of students that was part of his charm. I was uneasy when you married him, Lynne. I worried about you.'

'I wasn't seeing clearly in those days.' Lynne's smile was wry.

'We should have kept in touch. I never had your New York phone number. It wasn't listed,' Dan said.

'Bill insisted it was bad to have a

162

Manhattan listing. You got all kinds of crank calls,' Lynne explained.

'We'll keep in touch now,' Andrea promised.

'I was praying we'd find Bill and Susie with you,' Lynne said. 'The police refuse to take any action.'

'They can't,' Andrea pointed out compassionately. 'Not unless we give them a hook to use.' Lynne tried to interpret the silent communication between Dan and Andrea.

'First let's contact Bill's parents,' Dan began.

'Dan, they're both dead.' Lynne was startled. 'Don't you remember?'

'That was a story Bill circulated back at school. I never understood why. I assumed he'd told you the truth. They live up near the Vermont border. I've met them.'

Lynne gaped in astonishment.

'Bill told me his parents both died when he was nine. That he grew up in boarding schools in Arizona. That was the first tie between us. Our years in crummy boarding schools.' Lynne felt herself swathed in unreality. 'Bill said his father had been a philanderer who could never hold a job. He said his mother was an alcoholic who

163

beat him. He said they died together in a hotel fire.'

'Bill's parents are fine people.' Dan seemed upset that Bill had maligned his father and mother. 'They live in an 1837 farmhouse they bought while Bill was in high school. Bill and I drove up to visit them the Thanskgiving holiday of our senior year.'

'I remember when you two went away for that Thanksgiving weekend.' Lynne shook her head in incredulity.

'I had the weirdest feeling that Bill's parents were just a bit afraid of him. They love him,' Dan was quick to add. 'That shone from their eyes. He's an only child. A late child. But I'll wager he's put them through hell during his lifetime.'

'Bill told me you two were spending that long weekend with your parents.' Lynne was dazed by this tidal wave of revelations.

'My parents were out in California visiting my married sister. We drove up to visit his parents, planning to stay for the four day holiday. Then Bill decided to cut the visit short. We left Salem Friday night and went down to New York.' Dan grimaced in recall. 'I was sick at the way Bill treated those nice people. His contempt for them was unbelievable.'

'Susie's grandmother and grandfather.' Lynne was awed by this discovery. 'All these years Bill's deprived Susie of her grandparents.' A precious gift to Susie and to her.

'Bill hates his family. It started when his grandmother died. He was fifteen then. She left most of her estate to his father. Bill had been the doted-on only grandson. He'd expected a lot of money.'

'Then there was no lonely boarding school in Arizona?' Lynne was bewildered that Bill had lied so outrageously.

'Bill went to a private high school in Switzerland. That's where he learned to speak French and German so fluently. A boarding school.'

'Why did he go to school in Switzerland?' Andrea was curious.

'He never said. I suspect Bill was being difficult. Maybe his parents thought he'd benefit from a different type of schooling. European schools are usually much more disciplined.' Dan squinted in thought. 'Bill has a lot of hang-ups. Like in college.

He led an active social life. Lynne, you remember how girls chased after him. But I know he hated women.' Including her, Lynne, thought, and shivered. And Susie, who would one day be a woman.

'Why did you say that?' Ira demanded.

'When we used to go off-campus for a few beers on Friday evenings, Bill would cut out after a while and pick up a prostitute. It didn't matter that plenty of girls were available. He'd pay off the prostitute and then beat her. Once when he was drunk he boasted about how often this happened. Those stories almost broke up our friendship. But I told myself that Bill was lying.'

'Dan, how can we involve the police? With their files—with an APB—there's a chance he'd be picked up.' Andrea was concerned.

'You know their hands are tied unless we give them something to latch on to,' Dan said. 'We've got to contact Bill's parents. If we can dig up something in his past—some proof of violence, then I can go to some of my contacts and say, 'Look, this guy is potentially dangerous. It's on his record.'

It would be futile to say to the police,

'My husband beat me.' She had said it to the detective at the police precinct. But it was not part of the divorce proceedings. She was not on record as being an abused wife.

'You said Bill's parents live in Salem?' Ira leaned forward, anxious to move. 'Salem, Massachusetts?'

'No. Salem, New York. Not North Salem or South Salem, here in Westchester County,' Dan emphasised. 'Salem, New York, up along the Vermont border. It's about fifty miles north-east of Albany. A small, rural town. Maybe two thousand people.'

'Then there's probably only one family named Travers,' Lynne predicted.

'Let's try to reach them by phone,' Dan pursued. 'It'll be better if you call, Lynne. You can explain that you're Bill's wife.' For the moment they forgot that she wasn't. 'They probably don't know you exist.' His face softened. 'I'll bet they don't know they have a grandchild.'

'The downstairs phone is in there.' Andrea pointed to an open door across the centre hall. 'In the den.'

Lynne hurried into the den with Ira. Long-distance information gave her a number just outside the village of Salem, at a rural delivery address. The operator reported it was the only family named Travers in the Salem directory.

Lynne dialled. The operator interrupted the call.

'I'm sorry. There's trouble on this line. Will you please try the number at a later time?'

'When?' Lynne asked. Panic returning.

'In a few hours,' the operator apologised. 'There was a bad storm in the area last night. Some lines are down. We're sorry for the inconvenience.'

'Thank you.' Numbly, Lynne put down the phone.

'Their phone is out of order?' Ira asked.

'Lines are down in the area. They had a storm up there last night.' Dan and Andrea hung in the doorway, anxious to learn what had transpired. 'The operator said to try in a few hours.' Lynne grunted in frustration.

'How far is Salem from here?' Ira asked Dan.

'About 125 miles,' Dan guessed.

'I have a gut feeling we ought to drive up there and talk to Bill's parents,' Ira said.

Lynne was startled.

'Ira, 125 miles?' They couldn't afford that much time.

'We can be there in two and a half to three hours,' Ira pursued. 'Honey, it's the first real lead we've had.'

'If Bill's parents can provide proof that Bill is potentially dangerous, we'll have leverage with the police,' Dan said. 'They can move into action.'

'Will Bill's parents do that?' Andrea countered. 'You're talking about their only child.'

'They have a grandchild to protect,' Dan reminded gently. 'That's a powerful incentive.'

'I told Bill I'd be home most of the weekend.' Lynne stammered in her ambivalence. 'In case Susie suddenly became homesick. Suppose I'm all wrong about this? Suppose Bill *is* just trying to scare me? If Bill decides to bring Susie home early, I ought to be there.' Ira was talking about putting over 150 miles between them and the apartment.

'Try Bill's apartment again,' Andrea ordered. 'Then we'll figure which way to go.'

Lynne went back into the den to dial

Bill's number. She waited for ten rings. Was Bill there and just not answering? *Let him be there. Let Susie be safe.* Yet instinct told her Bill was not at home. Her husband was psychotic, and Susie was alone with him. *Where?*

'Hang up, honey,' Ira told her. 'Bill's not at the apartment.'

'Suppose he calls my apartment?' She ought to be there, even if only to receive his next vicious threat.

'Lynne, you drive up to Salem with Ira,' Andrea planned. 'Dan and I will go down to the city to cover the phone in your apartment. We'll make a tie-in with Jessica, so we'll know if Bill showed up at the zoo. If Bill calls, I'll explain that I'm a friend of yours from the office. I'm staying overnight because there was a fire in my building. You went off to the beach with Ira. I'll tell Bill to bring Susie to me. You can keep in touch by phone while you're driving up to Salem. You'll know if anything happens.'

'Lynne, we have to play it that way,' Ira told her.

'All right,' Lynne capitulated. 'We'll go to Salem.'

Chapter Sixteen

Bill swung off the Long Island Expressway at Exit 70. What a bastard of a trip on a hot Saturday like this, he thought in sullen anger. At least, the kid was asleep now. He didn't have to listen to all that yapping. Bitch, bitch, bitch. Like all females.

With the air conditioning off because the car was stalling, he propelled his way through sluggish traffic—cursing under his breath. He should have expected it this time of year.

Coming out here always reminded him of the old bitch. She should have left him more than the broken-down beach house. Some beach house, he jeered. Two miles from the ocean and falling apart.

Still, with the price of real estate out here he could pick up a bundle just for the land. Why the hell did he hang on to it? But he knew the answer to that. It was a place to run to when the hostile world got too hot.

Bill turned off the road, took a short-cut

into town. Then he was swinging into historic, tree-lined Job's Lane. An array of low-built, attractive stores stretched on both sides with the remembered aura of endlessness. Expensive boutiques, gourmet groceries, a fudge shop, exotic restaurants enticed passersby. He enjoyed the ambiance of Southampton, respected the image it created. Money and arrogance and high living. He'd like it better if he owned a million dollar ocean-front mansion.

Cars moved bumper-to-bumper in the usual summer season parade. Three months from now there'd be a handful of cars driving through here on a Saturday afternoon. Now the sidewalks were jammed with resort-clad humanity. At the outdoor dining area of The Driver's Seat people ate, indulged in fresh fruit daiquiris, and people-watched.

His eyes deserted the road for a moment to focus on the long, narrow, weather-shingled structure that was The Driver's Seat. No chance of dropping in for a Scotch on the rocks when he was tied down to the kid.

Then a feeling of pleasure filtered through him. The Seat was open until 4 a.m. Before 4 a.m., if he handled himself right, Susie would be receiving care in the Southampton hospital. He'd play the properly distraught father, then go to The Seat for a few drinks.

He'd figure a way to do it out at the house. Making sure nobody could lay a finger on him. Like the other times. With the house surrounded by woods the way it was, nobody even knew when he was there.

Lynne could carry on all she liked. It wouldn't mean a damn. The cops wouldn't be able to touch him. Everybody knew how careless little kids were. You read about freakish accidents all the time. This would be just one more.

'Daddy?' Susie stirred in wakefulness. 'Are we almost there?'

'We're in Southampton already.' A dozen tiny hammers pounded away at his head. A Scotch would have helped. 'We'll get to the house soon.'

'I'm hungry.' Susie was fretful.

'Okay, we'll eat before we go out to the house.' Maybe food would help his head. 'I'll have to find a place to park.'

With the car at last in a wedge of space within walking distance of the restaurant he had in mind, Bill prodded Susie back towards Job's Lane. They'd go into ACT IV for a sandwich. Whenever he stayed out here, he had breakfast at ACT IV.

Susie inspected the posters of Broadway productions that lined the walls of the cosy little restaurant. *Auntie Mame, Fiddler on the Roof, Rain.* Bill ordered turkey sandwiches and cokes for them. He leaned back in gratitude for the air conditioning.

He must have a clear head. No mistakes. Lynne had to pay for what she was doing to him. Wrecking his whole life. At the company Jim was a feudal lord. His word was law. Lynne knew that.

Bill devoured his sandwich with compulsive speed. He was irritated that Susie dawdled.

'Take the rest of the sandwich with you to the house,' he ordered after a restless few minutes and signalled to the waitress to bring them a doggie bag.

They pushed their way through the people-clogged streets to the car. Bill headed towards the house. Leaving fashionable Southampton behind them. His cottage had a Southampton address. Beyond that it had nothing in common with the resort town. He seethed with resentment every time he thought about his inheritance.

174

Hating his grandmother for denying him the bulk of her substantial estate.

He pulled up before a modest, paint-starved cottage that sat on a wooded half-acre plot. Tall pines screened it from neighbours on either side and to the rear. Opposite was a tiny, algae-covered pond.

'That's the house,' Bill said shortly, staring in distaste. He remembered the summer his grandmother tacked on the deck. He had been about six. It was supposed to be a place for him to play. Stupid, putting a deck on something that looked like a broken-down farmhouse. Bill reached over to open the door for Susie. 'Get out.'

'Daddy, you said you'd buy me a doll when we got out here,' Susie reminded him aggrievedly. Her small face was tear-blotched. Her mouth bore the residue of chocolate frozen yogurt.

'Later we'll buy the doll.' He prodded her towards the stairs that led to the deck. 'Before we go out to dinner.'

They would go over to Herb McCarthy's. He'd have the roast duckling, he decided. They made it real crisp. Just the way he liked it. Susie and he would eat out on the porch. It'd be cool in the evening.

After dinner he'd take her back to the house. Then he'd do it. On a Saturday night when the whole town was swinging. And he'd keep that date with The Seat.

'Can we swim in the pond over there?' Susie paused to inspect the greenish oval of water.

For an instant Bill churned with excitement. He could see Susie walking into the pond. It was shallow at the sides. She didn't know it was seven feet deep in the middle.

No, he rejected mentally. Annoyed with himself for considering this. He didn't want Susie to drown. That would be too easy for Lynne. He'd made up his mind when he walked out of Lynne's apartment with Susie. He wanted Lynne to suffer for the next fifty years.

'Daddy?' Susie repeated. 'Can we swim in the pond?'

'No. The water's too dirty.'

He knew exactly how to do it. And he had to do it tonight.

Chapter Seventeen

While Ira and Dan conferred over a New York state map, Lynne telephoned Jessica. The two men were trying to pinpoint the shortest route to Salem.

'I want to avoid the throughway,' Ira said. 'It'll be loaded today. I think the fastest way would be to head straight up Route 22. It'll take us directly into Salem.'

'Route 22 cuts through a stream of small towns,' Dan cautioned. 'Your speed gets cut down.'

'But on a hot summer weekend everybody will be on the parkways,' Ira reminded him. 'We'll make better time on 22.'

Lynne explained the situation to Jessica and got off the phone. With luck on their side they'd be talking to Bill's parents in less than three hours. Three hours, her mind taunted, when every minute she feared for Susie's well-being.

Ira rose to his feet with car keys in hand.

'Let's go, Lynne.' His eyes were sympathetic. He knew her agony. How would she survive this without Ira?

As they headed north on route 22, Lynne checked her watch again. It was 3.50 p.m. Susie had been alone with Bill for almost twenty-two hours.

Bill's threats ricocheted through Lynne's mind. Let Susie be all right. Let them find her before Bill did something unspeakable. She felt sick. What fresh insanity was fomenting in his mind?

As Ira had expected, traffic on 22 was light. Route 22, lined with lush summer greenery, cut through a stream of rural towns. A skilful driver, Ira drove as fast as conditions permitted, closing his eyes to the speed limit except when the route was interrupted by inhabited areas; watching for police cars that might pull him off and cost precious minutes they could ill afford.

From exhaustion Lynne dozed at intervals, awaking with a guilty start to confront the nightmare that had imprisoned her since yesterday at shortly past 6 p.m.

'Do you want to stop and call the apartment?' Ira asked when they had been on the road for well over an hour. 'Andrea

178

and Dan must have arrived by now. We need gas, anyway.'

'Please,' Lynne whispered. She hated to waste time, but she needed to touch base. And Ira had said they needed gas.

They watched the road for a gas station with a telephone. When Ira spied one, they pulled off. While Ira gassed up the car, Lynne phoned her apartment. Andrea and Dan had arrived and had spoken with Jessica. No word from anybody, Andrea reported.

Had Bill tried to reach her? But he couldn't expect her to sit by the phone all day. Would he? He was smart enough to know that if she went to the police, she'd get no action. A domestic squabble. That's what the detective had called it.

Lynne returned to the car. Ira was checking the tires. One needed air. Within minutes they were back on the road. Her throat constricted at the sight of two small girls selling corn from behind a card table on a patch of sun-parched lawn. The smaller one had dark hair that fell almost to her waist. Like Susie's, before Bill took a scissor to it.

No three-hour span in her lifetime had seemed so excruciatingly long. She realised, too, that this could be yet another wild goose chase. Yet Dan, with his sharp legal mind, had pinpointed this as their best lead. Bill's parents held the key to police involvement.

'We should be pulling into Salem soon,' Ira comforted her as they drove through the little town of Cambridge. 'I think it's about another ten miles.' He reached for the map he had shoved behind him. 'Check it out.' He was keeping her busy to ease the agony of waiting, Lynne interpreted.

She inspected the map, searched to locate Cambridge. Here. She followed the line that was Route 22 to Salem. Now she conferred with the scale.

'It is about ten miles,' she confirmed.

Lynne kept her eyes riveted to the roadside. Watching for a sign that would indicate they were approaching Salem.

'Village of Salem,' Lynne announced. 'There's a plaque about some Revolutionary battle.'

They drove past a series of neat, modest houses, then stopped at the first traffic light in a long stretch.

'This is Salem,' Ira said with an air of optimism. 'We're on the main street. Let's park and go ask directions.' The only address they had was a rural delivery number, acquired from the telephone operator.

Ira parked off Main Street beside an ice cream store on the corner. Across the way was the local library and the firehouse. Just ahead of them, next to what Lynne believed were two old Federal houses, was the modern brick post office.

'Ira, it's so quiet.' The streets were deserted. The stores closed.

'Honey, it's past seven on a Saturday evening,' Ira told her. 'In small towns stores keep short hours.' His eyes skimmed the area around them. 'Let's try that place. They're open.' He nodded towards the ice cream store. A. Stewart's.

The clerks at Stewart's were friendly but unfamiliar with local people. Both said they came from Greenwich.

'Try the tavern down the street,' a long-haired youth behind the counter suggested. 'They'll probably be able to help you.'

They walked to the immaculate white clapboard structure that housed a tavern and a restaurant. Again they found friendliness but no information.

'Ira, somebody here has to know them,' Lynne said in desperation. Her eyes scanned the other side of the street. 'There's Grand Union. Let's see if they're open.'

'Wait.' Ira reached for her hand and pulled her along with him.

A jovial-faced man in his forties was locking up the door of a double-windowed store set above low, wide stairs. A plaque on the wall of the three-storied building indicated it was a historic landmark.

'Could you help us, please?' Ira called out, and the man turned to them with a quick, warm smile.

'Sure will, if I can,' he said leisurely.

'We're looking for a family,' Ira explained. 'Their telephone is out of order—'

'Oh, a lot of phones are down since the storm last night. It was a lulu. What's their name?'

'Travers,' Ira said, and the man's face lit up in recognition.

'Oh yeah. The Travers have been here for about twelve or fourteen years. Fine people. Keep pretty much to themselves,' he continued, 'though Mr Travers helps out on the Rescue Squad. They live out on West Hebron. Up the hill a piece. You a stranger in the area?' he enquired with an air of wishing to be helpful.

'Yes, we are.' Lynne churned to be at the Travers' house.

'Make a right at the light. That takes you out onto West Broadway. That merges into West Hebron, but don't expect to see any sign saying so,' he warned, chuckling. 'The house is about a mile and a quarter from the traffic light. Just keep straight ahead, up a kinda sharp hill. You'll see a nice-looking old brick house at the crest, then a white development-type house, and after that a red farmhouse set back from the road. Just across the way from the farmhouse is the Travers place. It's red, too, with white shutters. An 1837 clipboard. Folks around here say that it was a stop on the Underground Railroad before the Civil War.'

'Thanks for the directions.' Ira smiled in gratitude.

'My pleasure.' The storekeeper raised a hand in farewell. 'You'll see the Travers' name on the mailbox at the edge of the road just across from the house. The mail boxes are all on the other side,' he called after them.

Ira drove straight ahead as instructed. Lynne's eyes clung to the road. Watching for the landmarks. They pulled up onto the crest of the hill. Lynne spied the pleasant old brick house on the right. Then a white ranch above a manicured lawn. Beyond it the red farmhouse behind towering elms. And on the left the red, white-shuttered clapboard that must be the Travers home.

Ira pulled up before the mailbox across from the house. 'Travers' was spelled out in neat gold letters.

'No lights in the house,' Lynne noticed, her stomach churning again.

'It's early. The sun's still out. There's no need for lights yet,' Ira encouraged.

Bill's parents lived here. The parents she had thought long dead. Susie's *grandparents*. All at once she felt less alone in the world. For Susie she had worried that there were no grandparents, no aunts and uncles and cousins to complete her world. The half-uncle in California—her father's child by his second marriage—was lost to her. Her father's third family somewhere in South America strangers—who spoke a foreign language. But here Susie had *grandparents*.

'Let's drive up to the house,' Ira said gently and pulled into the driveway.

At one end of the gravel driveway was a fenced-in area serving as a corral for two horses. Ahead of them a cottontail hopped into the grass. They left the car and crossed to the small, screened-in porch. A huge calico cat dozed on the pillowed seat of a sturdy rocker. The door to the porch had been left ajar. Purposely, Lynne suspected, so that the cat could come up here whenever he wished.

Ira rang the bell. They could hear the chimes echoing inside. No sound of anyone walking to the door. Lynne's heart pounded. Ira rang again.

'They don't seem to be home,' Ira admitted after a few moments. 'Let's go ask at the house across the road. They may know when the Travers are due back.'

'They have to come home to feed the horses. And the cat.' Lynne was breathless with anxiety.

'I'll ask next door.'

They went to the car. Ira followed the circular driveway behind the house and around to the other side.

A boy of about eleven stood there, gazing inquiringly at them.

'Do you know when the Travers will be home?' Ira called from the car. Let them not be away for the weekend, Lynne prayed.

185

The boy sauntered across the lawn to them. One of the horses whinnied.

'Mr and Mrs Travers went over to some fair across county this morning,' the boy reported. 'They won't be coming home till late tonight. I came over to feed the horses and Rasputin. That's the cat.'

'What do you call late?' Ira wanted to know.

'Mr Travers said they might not be home till midnight. After the fair they were going to some concert at the Performing Arts Centre. That's over at Saratoga.'

'Thank you,' Ira said while Lynne bit her lip in disappointment.

'Oh, Ira. To be so close,' Lynne whispered while they moved out onto the road again.

'We'll stay up here until we can talk to them.' Ira was decisive. 'Even if it means staying at a motel for the night and talking to them in the morning.'

Lynne stared at him in shock. Ira was saying they might not find Susie until tomorrow? How could they know what might happen to Susie overnight?

'How can we just sit and wait?' she protested, battling against hysteria. 'There has to be something else—'

186

'The Travers hold the key.' Ira's face was taut. 'We *have* to talk with them.'

'But suppose Bill calls the apartment?' she stammered, her mind in chaos. This wasn't real—it was a nightmare.

'Dan and Andrea are there. They're prepared to stay the night. Honey, we can't do anything in the city. It's important to talk with Bill's parents,' he reiterated.

'Can we find a phone so I can call the apartment?' Lynne struggled to control her trembling. She had never felt so lost, so scared, in her whole life. So helpless, when Susie desperately needed her.

'You'll phone the apartment,' Ira soothed. One hand left the wheel to grasp hers for a moment. 'We'll stop somewhere to eat. It won't help Susie for you to fall apart.'

They searched Main Street for a public phone. They discovered one in front of the Grand Union. But this phone, too, was out of order.

'I noticed a restaurant as we were approaching Salem,' Ira recalled. 'They'll have a phone. There were motel units there, too. Watch for a log cabin on the left.'

They located the Log Cabin about three miles beyond Salem. Inside the restaurant Lynne went instantly to the phone, located near the door, while Ira groped for change. An arm comfortingly at her waist, he waited while she dialled her apartment number.

Andrea answered on the first ring. Nothing had happened at that end. Jessica had called to check with them when the zoo closed for the day. Lynne reported what had occurred at the Travers' house.

'At least you know the Travers are not away on vacation.' Andrea sounded relieved at this development. 'You're staying up there?'

'Ira thinks we should.' Now Lynne was ambivalent.

'Wait a minute. Talk to Dan.'

Lynne heard Andrea and Dan in discussion at the other end. Then Dan was on the phone.

'Lynne, I agree with Ira. Stick with the Travers. Let me talk to Ira for a minute.'

Lynne stood by while Dan talked and Ira listened. Then Ira hung up and prodded her towards a table by the window, overlooking a pond across the road.

'What did Dan say?'

'That we should stay on the track of Bill's parents and dig up information he can take

188

to the police.' Like Bill's psychiatric history, Lynne understood.

'I hope we're doing the right thing—' A fresh tide of helplessness rode over her. So far from home when they didn't know where Susie was. Didn't know if she was all right.

'We'll have dinner, then check into the motel.' Ira was trying to sound matter-of-fact, but a hint of apprehension crept through.

'How can I stay away from the apartment overnight?' Her precarious hold on reality was failing.

'It may not be necessary,' Ira comforted. 'We may see the Travers tonight. But this is a weekend. We must make sure we have a place to stay if the Travers don't come back till too late to talk to them. And we'll have a phone where Dan and Andrea can reach us,' he soothed.

'Can't we just wait at the house until Bill's parents return?'

'We're asking them to incriminate their son,' Ira said compassionately. 'They'll be better able to face that at 7 in the morning than at 2 a.m. We can't bungle this, Lynne.'

'But to waste all those hours—' Her

voice soared perilously.

'Honey, this is our best shot. You mustn't let yourself come unglued now. We need the Travers, but we can't approach them when they're exhausted and too tired to think clearly. We can't hang around much past midnight.'

'I keep thinking, maybe Bill will call and I can talk to him.' But what could she say that would change Bill into a rational human being?

'Lynne, you can't talk to him,' Ira said. 'Dan has been in touch with the Manhattan police. Using his professional contacts. If we can bring in proof that Bill has a record of physical violence, they're empowered to move instantly. But it has to be concrete proof,' he warned. 'Dan's convinced Bill must have some adolescent record of violence. He figures that's why his parents shipped him off to school in Switzerland.'

'You expect the Travers to give us that proof?'

'For Susie's sake—for their grandchild—I think they will. There's a hell of a lot about Bill you don't know. That business of his beating up prostitutes. I don't think Dan believed that until you admitted Bill had beat you. Why did the Travers send him to school in Switzerland?' he reiterated. 'They're not jet set rich. It must have been a financial hardship.'

'Bill's been gone with Susie for over twenty-four hours. I'm scared. I've never been so scared in my whole life.'

'We have to hang in there, Lynne. We'll reach the Travers. We'll make them help us.'

Lynne forced herself to eat because Ira was so solicitous. He ordered the roast turkey dinner for them at their waitress's suggestion. Lynne was amazed at the enormous amount of food placed before them in a matter of minutes.

The other diners about them ate with gusto. But tonight food was repugnant to Lynne.

Chapter Eighteen

Bill left Susie asleep in the lower segment of the maple bunk bed in the smaller bedroom and drove down to the liquor store for a bottle of Scotch. As soon as

Susie woke up, they'd go over to Herb McCarthy's for dinner.

From the liquor store he cut over to the supermarket for ice cubes because the ancient refrigerator in the house took forever to freeze them. At the checkout counter he picked up a copy of *Gentlemen's Quarterly*.

When he returned, he found Susie was still asleep. he looked down at her with simmering rage, the recurrent question charging through his brain. Whose little bastard had Lynne palmed off as his?

He wheeled about to the other bedroom. He wasn't sure just yet exactly how to do it. After dinner he'd sit down—his head clear—and figure out the details.

He fixed himself a Scotch on the rocks and lounged across the country maple sofa, scanning *Gentlemen's Quarterly* while he drank. He had to get rid of some of these pressures. Then he'd feel better.

He couldn't square things with Jim, but he could make life miserable for Lynne. He had to make his move in just the right way. No slip-ups.

A surge of confidence welled in him. *He never slipped up.* His folks thought they knew what had happened that summer when he was fifteen. That was why they rushed him off to Switzerland. But they couldn't prove it. The cops couldn't touch him. They wouldn't touch him this time, either.

Whistling he went out to the kitchen and made himself another drink, returned to the sofa in the living room. When they reached the restaurant, he'd phone Lynne again. Remind her what could happen when a little girl went too far out into the ocean. He wouldn't do it that way—but let Lynne sweat some more.

'Daddy?'

Susie stood in the doorway. Tiny and forlorn.

'You want to go out to eat now?' Bill consulted his watch. It was almost 8.30. At this hour on a Saturday night they'd have to wait for a table.

'You said you'd buy me a doll,' she reproached. 'As big as me.'

'You slept too late. The stores are closed. We'll buy it tomorrow. Let's go out to dinner now.'

'But you promised me a doll,' Susie insisted. Tired and apprehensive.

'I told you, the stores are closed,' he yelled and she hunched her small shoulders in alarm. 'Tomorrow we'll buy the doll,' he repeated. 'That's a promise.'

Tomorrow she wouldn't be in the mood to go shopping for a doll. She'd be lying in a bed in the Southampton hospital with a team of doctors fussing over her. He'd call Lynne to get the hell out here to see her precious baby.

Tonight, he swore, reaching for his third Scotch on the rocks. No more stalling. Tonight he'd do it. Over dinner he'd figure out the details.

Bill parked the car and with Susie at his side walked up to the porch of the expansive white structure that was Herb McCarthy's landmark restaurant. Waiting in line for a table he fidgeted, annoyed at the admiring gazes Susie was garnering from other patrons. They didn't expect to see a little kid here at this hour. But this would work out to his advantage, his mind pinpointed.

'We'll get a table in a few minutes, baby.' He reached for one small hand. Switching on the charm that had been missing all day. If anything went wrong—if Lynne tried to make trouble—let all these people here see—and tell the cops—that he was devoted to his pretty little daughter.

'Daddy, I want to go home.' She lifted wistful eyes to his. 'I want to see Mommie.'

'Baby, don't you like this place?' He reached down to swoop her up into his arms. 'I'm taking you out to a fancy restaurant just like you were a grown-up lady.'

'It's all right.'

'We'll order the roast duckling. You'll like that. Then for dessert, chocolate mousse cake. It's sensational.'

'Okay.' But she squirmed in his arms.

At last Bill and Susie were seated at a table on the porch, beneath the colourful array of lanterns. He concentrated on lifting Susie's spirits. Let everybody notice what a devoted father he was.

Susie responded to his efforts. By the time the chocolate mousse cake arrived, she was effervescent. Bill prided himself on bringing this off. He'd take her to the house from here and put her to bed. Then he'd sit down and draw up his plans. Dinner had cleared his head.

Before they left the restaurant Bill sought out the bank of telephone booths. He had promised himself he'd call Lynne again from McCarthy's. Give her fresh cause to sweat. He had no phone at the house. He'd have to call from here.

Dropping coins into the slot at the operator's request he envisioned Lynne sacked out with Ira. The phone would ring. She'd get out of bed and hear his little piece. She'd be too sick to let that creep touch her again.

'Hello.' An unfamiliar feminine voice greeted him on the first ring. He started. Who the hell was that? Without a word he hung up.

He stood immobile at the phone. His mind in a jumble. The operator must have given him the wrong number. Call her and tell her! Tell her to get it right this time.

Despite the coolness of the restaurant he was perspiring as he laboured to put through another call. Again the phone rang. Again it was picked up on the first ring.

'Hello.' The same feminine voice responded.

Bill hung up. Where the hell was Lynne? Did she go to the police? Was that a policewoman on the phone? The police couldn't do anything. No crime had been committed.

Had Lynne brought in the police? She shouldn't have done that.

By the time Bill and Susie returned to the house, she was asleep again. Bill carried her inside and dropped her onto the lower section of the bunk bed. His mind was in chaos. He was in a cold sweat. Lynne should have been at the apartment to listen to him. *Lynne, do you know how easy it is for a little girl to drown if she goes out into the ocean alone? One big wave comes in, washes her out, and it's all over.* That was what he would say to her.

Swearing under his breath Bill stalked out to the kitchen to fix himself another drink. That damn little slut must have run to the cops. But it wouldn't do her any good. They'd figure her for just another crazy woman mad at her ex. The cops wouldn't do a thing.

But he would.

Chapter Nineteen

Lynne and Ira finished dinner at the Log Cabin. They drove the minuscule distance from the restaurant to the small, unpretentious motel. Lynne stayed in the car while Ira went to check in.

It was crazy to be staying up here all night, she thought with fresh doubts. She ought to be in New York. At the apartment. In reach if Bill phoned. Maybe this time she could talk to him. But logic told her to listen to Ira and Dan.

Ira emerged from the office with a key in hand.

'We're right here,' he said, opening the car door and pointing to the unit facing the car.

'Ira, are you sure we ought to check in?' she hedged. If we talk to the Travers, we'll drive right back to the city.' Hopefully with facts to take to the police.

'On a summer Saturday night in a resort area, motels are apt to be full up. We have to make sure to have a room if we stay overnight,' he pointed out gently.

Ira pushed the door wide and flipped on a switch, then drew Lynne into their unit. A lamp on the dresser offered muted illumination. Her eyes settled on the telephone beside the bed.

'I'll call the apartment and tell Andrea and Dan where we are.' The telephone was their lifeline.

She sat at the edge of the bed and reached for the phone. She read the instruction for making calls. Her shoulders ached with tension; her eyes burned from lack of sleep. She dialled and heard the ring at the other end. Heard it ring again. And again.

'Hello.' Andrea picked up on the fourth ring. She sounded out of breath.

'Andrea, we're at a motel about three miles south of Salem. Here's the number.' She read off the number on the circlet within the dial. 'The area code is 518.'

'Got it,' Andrea said. 'Lynne, don't be upset, but somebody called. Whoever it was hung up. Then he dialled a second time, as though he suspected he'd dialled a wrong number the first time. He hung up again without saying a word.'

'Bill,' Lynne guessed. Ira sat down beside

her to drop a reassuring arm about her shoulders. 'It must have been Bill. I should have been there!' She turned to Ira. 'Bill called. We have to go back to New York!'

'Wait.' Ira took the phone from her and spoke to Andrea. 'Did the caller say anything?' He listened for an instant. 'I think we have to stay here. Bill's parents are our only real contact.' He paused. 'Sure, Andrea.' He turned to Lynne. 'Dan's at the door. He'd gone downstairs to make some calls. He didn't want to tie up this line. I'm holding on.'

Ira talked to Dan now. Lynne sensed a fresh excitement in him.

'Dan, that's great!'

'What's happening?' Lynne demanded as Ira put down the phone.

'Dan's located a friend who's a private investigator. The guy is coming right over to hook up some equipment to the phone. If Bill calls again—and if they can keep him talking long enough—they'll be able to trace the call.'

'Why didn't Dan do that before Bill made the last call?' Lynne was querulous in despair; forgetting that Bill had hung up without uttering a word.

'Andrea said Dan's been trying for hours, at a phone downstairs, to reach a guy who'd be willing to do this for him. It's not exactly acceptable to the police.' His smile was wry.

'How will they make Bill talk if he calls again?' Lynne battled a compulsion to rush back to the city.

'I don't know.' Ira was honest. 'But if it's humanly possible, Dan and Andrea will do it.'

Ira reached to massage the taut muscles between her shoulder blades. Lynne closed her eyes, abandoning herself to the relief his hands wrought. The terrible heat of the day had diminished with stunning swiftness. A chill settling down about the room now.

'We may have rain before the night's over,' Ira commented, gazing through the window at the darkening sky.

'I hope it doesn't storm.' Fresh anxiety gripped her. 'Susie's terrified of lightning.'

'It won't be a storm,' Ira guessed. 'They had a bad storm up here last night.'

That was why the Travers' phone was out, Lynne remembered.

'Ira, do you think Susie's all right?'

Compulsively she questioned him. Irrationally, she rebuked herself in a corner of her mind. 'Will we find them before Bill—before he does something awful?'

'We'll find them,' Ira promised; knowing nothing. How could they know? Lynne tormented herself. 'Stretch out and rest a while.' He prodded her back against the pillows and crossed to close the drapes.

Ira lay down beside her, drawing her to him in comfort. His arm protective, his closeness a reassurance that her world might not have fallen completely apart.

For a little while she dozed. She awoke to faint sounds at the door.

'Ira?' Now she realised he wasn't beside her.

'I went for coffee.' He was coming into the room. 'We'll have the coffee and then drive over to the Travers' house.'

'Is it that late?' Lynne was astonished; guilty that she had slept.

'No, but a heavy fog is settling over the roads. I want to be sure we find the house. We'll have to drive slowly.' He sat beside her and deposited two containers of coffee on the night table. 'Drink this while it's hot.'

She was grateful for the warmth of the

coffee. Only now did she realise she was shivering from the chill.

'I checked in the trunk of the car to see if Andrea and Dan had left a blanket or something back there. I found a sweater.' He draped a pale blue cardigan about her shoulders as she drank.

In minutes they were in the car and back on Route 22, on their way to Salem. Fog hung low over the pond across from the motel and over the fields ahead where corn was growing tall. Unseasonable coolness in the air. Ira reached to switch on the car heater.

'Saturday night is accident night in small towns like this,' Ira said as they passed a bar, and Lynne flinched. 'Too many drinks at a gin mill and somebody ploughs into a telephone pole.' He was suddenly aware of her agitation. 'Lynne, I didn't mean to talk about accidents.'

'I know.' She tried to brush ugly images from her mind.

'Smell the birch logs burning in a fireplace?' Ira sniffed appreciatively. 'Are you warm enough, honey?'

'I'm fine.' Was Susie fine?

They drove into town. The traffic light was now a blinker. Ira turned left on West

Broadway that would merge into West Hebron. Most of the houses in town were unlit. Moving beyond the town limits they saw the fields shrouded in fog. Somewhere a hound dog barked.

'Somebody's out hunting tonight,' Ira said, and again a chill invaded Lynne despite the warmth inside the car.

They reached the crest of the hill. Lynne leaned forward, praying to see a light in the Travers house. Two windows of the brick house on the right were illuminated. The white ranch was dark. From the red farmhouse—where one room was lighted—came a haunting orchestral performance of Beethoven's *Moonlight Sonata*. Across the way the Travers' house was dark and silent.

'We'll park here at the side of the road and wait,' Ira said.

The residents of the farmhouse on the right turned off their stereo. The room went dark. A few moments later a light shone briefly in a room at the far end of the house.

An occasional car came along the road. At the sound of each approaching motor Ira flicked on the lights to warn of their presence. A motorcycle charged down the road, splintering the quietness of the night.

At 12.30 a.m. Ira capitulated. He was wary of approaching the Travers at a disturbingly late hour. That might put them off, he warned Lynne.

'Lynne, we must have their help. We can't approach them at 2 a.m.' His smile was wry. 'Even midnight is late for an unscheduled call.'

'Can't Dan do something to push the police?' Lynne asked in a fresh surge of desperation. 'He's a lawyer. He knows judges and detectives.'

'The police can't go against the law,' Ira said patiently. 'We have to bring Dan something he can use. We'll be back here at 7 a.m. We'll wait till the Travers are awake. We'll make them understand the urgency of the situation.'

'How do I know what's happening to Susie right this minute?' Lynne's voice was shrill with terror. 'How do I know something won't happen during the night? Bill's a night person. He can stay up till five in the morning and be wide awake at eight. He brags about how he can get along on three hours' sleep a night.'

'Lynne, we'll find Susie.' Ira reached for her hand. She felt his strength. Oh

God, she wanted to believe him! 'Hold on to that.'

Ira turned into the Travers' driveway, backed out, and swung around in the direction that would take them back to the motel. Lynne's eyes clung to the road, praying a car would approach that would be occupied by an older couple. The Travers.

But no car passed.

Chapter Twenty

Bill awoke with a suddenness that almost threw him off the sofa. His half-finished drink sat watered down on the coffee table. He looked at the sunburst clock on the wall and grunted in disgust. It was almost 1 a.m.

What the hell was the matter with him? He should have had the job done by now. The kid should be lying in a hospital bed and he should be on a bar stool in The Driver's Seat. Wasn't that what he'd promised himself when they drove into town?

He picked up his glass and walked into the kitchen to fix himself a fresh drink. God, he hated everything about this stinking house. Who but his grandmother would furnish a beach house in country maple?

He settled himself in the chintz-covered rocker flanking the sofa. All right. Dig in. How was he going to do it? The plan had to be foolproof. He had to come out of this smelling like a rose.

Involuntarily his mind hurtled back through the years. To the summer of his fifteenth birthday. Not long after the old lady croaked. He was pissed off at the way she had screwed him in her will...

It was a muggy July evening in the mildly affluent community of Cranston Hills, about eighteen miles above Albany. Almost midnight. His folks were asleep. They thought he was asleep. Tomorrow was a school day.

His folks never suspected the nights he prowled the sleep-logged neighbourhood. He didn't need to sleep like other people. Three hours' sleep and he was ready to go again.

The houses were dark on both sides of the street as he strutted down Sycamore

Lane. The moon was a chunk of pale yellow hanging in the sky, the air pungent with the scent of roses. Close by two tomcats were battling; the only sounds in the night. He felt himself king of the universe walking alone this way on the deserted street.

Ahead of him he saw the light in a side window of old Miss McDougall's house. He hated Miss McDougall. She used to play bridge every Friday night with his grandmother and two other old biddies. She'd cried at the funeral.

He slowed down as he approached Miss McDougall's neat, white colonial house. He didn't want to talk to her. Through the foliage he saw her small spare figure at the side door. She was letting out that old tabby cat she spoiled rotten.

'You hurry back, Mehitabel,' Miss McDougall's high-pitched voice echoed through the silence. 'I want to get to bed.'

Bill heard Mehitabel meow as she scampered over the grass. The kitchen went dark. A light was turned on in the dining room. He cursed under his breath when the cat brushed up against him.

'Shut up.' His grandmother used to save

meat and chicken scraps for Mehitabel.
Sometimes she cornered him into taking
a bag of food over to Miss McDougall for
that stupid cat. 'Shut up!'

Suddenly he could see his grandmother
fussing over Mehitabel. She wouldn't get
another cat after hers died, but she loved
this bitch.

'Meow.' Mehitabel was indignant when
his sneakered foot hit her in the shank.

'Didn't I tell you to shut up?' He hated
that damn cat.

In a torrent of rage he reached to pick
her up. His hands tightened about her
neck. She clawed wildly for a moment,
then hung limp from his hands.

'Mehitabel?' Miss McDougall's voice was
anxious. He hadn't noticed that the kitchen
light was on again. She was standing right
in the doorway in a spill of brightness.
'Mehitabel? What are you carrying on
about?'

She spied Mehitabel dangling from Bill's
hands.

'Oh, my God!'

Before a scream could emerge from her
throat, he dropped Mehitabel and lunged
forward. He had to shut her up.

Her arms moved convulsively as he

squeezed out her life. Then, like Mehitabel, she hung limp. He released her, watched her body fall to the ground.

His eyes were galvanised to the body at his feet. It was his grandmother he had just killed. He surged with an orgiastic pleasure.

Miss McDougall's body wasn't found until the next morning when the milkman made his delivery. He found her and the cat side by side. The whole community was stunned. They were sure she had been robbed. Only the police admitted, later, that nothing was missing. Miss McDougall had not been raped. They couldn't figure out a motive.

Once a month for the next four months another old lady in their community died in the same way. The life choked from her. The cops came up with nothing. They kept hauling in suspects, letting them go for lack of evidence.

Every old lady in the area was petrified. Nobody went out at night. They didn't play bridge. They didn't go out to dinner. They didn't visit. Some of the women who lived alone moved in with their married sons or daughters. Others left town. Once a month he felt the kind of pleasure that killing old Miss McDougall had given him.

But then his parents got suspicious. He never understood why. But they never came right out and accused him. They were scared of him. And then they dragged him off to that rotten place in Switzerland.

Chapter Twenty-One

Dressed except for shoes, Lynne lay sleepless beneath the light blanket provided by the motel. Beside her Ira slept with one arm protectively across her shoulders. They had remained dressed because Lynne wanted to be prepared to run at any call from Dan and Andrea.

Lynne struggled to see the face of her watch without disturbing Ira. The early morning cold was penetrating. More like late autumn than July. Her watch confirmed the greyness of dawn that seeped between the drapes. It was almost 5 a.m.

Cautiously Lynne extricated herself from Ira's arm and left the bed. En route to the window she reached for the cardigan that lay across a chair and pulled it on. Lifting a corner of the drapes she saw the thick fog that hung low over the pond across the road.

Sunday morning. In towns like this all over the country, families would soon be waking to a normal morning free of workday care. To what was she waking? What nightmare was Bill conjuring up for Susie and her?

Bill had walked out of the house with Susie almost thirty-five hours before. Where were they? Was Susie all right? How many times had she asked herself these questions in the past thirty-five hours?

In thirteen hours the police could move in if Bill didn't bring Susie back. But what would happen to Susie in those thirteen hours? What had happened? Was Susie terrified? Poor, sweet baby. Was she crying for 'Mommie'?

Tortured by uncertainty Lynne remained at the window, gazing without seeing through the narrow opening of the drapes while the dark greyness outdoors brightened into morning.

'How long have you been awake?' Ira pulled himself into a sitting position. 'Did you sleep at all?'

'A little. I just got out of bed. It's cold.'
She pulled the cardigan together at her
throat.

'We'll go look for a place to have an
early breakfast.' Ira swung his feet to the
floor. 'Just give me five minutes for a fast
shower.'

The Log Cabin was not yet open for
breakfast. They drove to Cambridge in
search of a diner that might be serving
this early on a Sunday morning.

'You'll feel better with some hot food
in you.' Ira scanned the roadside for
indications of a restaurant ready to receive
patrons.

They stopped at the sight of a rugged,
weatherbeaten old man walking a dog and
asked about where they might find a place
to eat at this time of morning.

'On Sundays most places are closed,' he
said with an air of apology. He frowned
in thought while the dog pulled at the
leash, so unexpected in these surroundings.
'Wait. I do know a diner that opens at 5
a.m. on Sundays.'

Lynne and Ira followed his directions to
a small diner, its windows steamed over
in cosy warmth. The only patrons were a
pair of good-humoured truckers sitting at

213

the counter. Ira piloted Lynne to a table at the rear. A tanned young waitress came over to take their order.

Despite Lynne's protests Ira ordered orange juice, ham and eggs, toast and coffee for each of them.

'You have to eat.' He reached to cover one of her hands with his. 'It'll help pass the time,' he added.

Like on planes, Lynne thought. The stewardesses were always throwing trays of food at you. To stop you from realising you were thousands of feet above the earth.

Their orange juice arrived. Freshly squeezed. Along with the juice the waitress brought a plate piled high with hot country biscuits.

'To hold you till your ham and eggs come.' Her smile was ingenuous and friendly. The waitress couldn't know the agony that gnawed at her, Lynne thought.

Lynne ate without tasting. At regular intervals her eyes moved to the wall clock. Would the Travers be early risers? But they couldn't go up and ring the doorbell at six in the morning. Not when the Travers had been out so late. Not with what they had to say.

Ira reached into his pocket for coins. He had spied a public phone in the rear.

'I'll call the apartment,' he said after he had signalled the waitress to bring him a refill of coffee. 'We ought to let Dan and Andrea know that we're away from the motel.'

'Right.' She forced a shaky smile.

What had Bill thought when he discovered somebody else in the apartment? He must realise she wouldn't sit by and do nothing while he threatened Susie. Had she pushed him into taking some ugly action when, in truth, he had only been trying to frighten her?

Ira had reached Dan and Andrea. He was talking to them. She knew from his replies that nothing had occurred. Bill had not tried to reach her again. There had been no phone call to trace.

Ira returned to their table as the waitress arrived with their food. He was silent until they were alone again.

'No word.' He confirmed her suspicion. 'Let's eat and drive back to Salem. Maybe the Travers are early risers.'

Lynne and Ira left the diner. The sun was striving to push through the early morning fog. No one walked on the street. Not a car moved. Somewhere in the distance church bells tolled.

They climbed into the car and headed north for Salem.

'This is beautiful country,' Ira said while they drove along the empty road. His eyes swept appreciatively from one side to the other. 'Those mountains over there must be Vermont. I skied up above Manchester a couple of years ago,' he recalled. 'That must be about twenty-five miles from here. And I understand there's great fishing in this area. One of the best streams in the country for trout. The Battenkill, I think.'

Ira was talking to try to keep her mind off Susie. Didn't he know that was impossible? Her baby's life was in danger. How could she think of anything else?

They pulled up at the side of the road, just before the Travers house. This morning the horses were not in view. Then they heard a whinny and spied both horses cantering in the field behind the house.

'The Travers are probably still asleep,' Ira guessed and Lynne sighed in disappointment. The shades across the front of the house were drawn. At the kitchen

216

windows half-shutters topped by curtains closed off the sight of the interior. 'They got home awfully late last night,' he reminded Lynne.

'I smell coffee.' Lynne sniffed, her mind racing. 'Ira, it *is* coffee. They must be awake!' She turned to him in supplication.

'Honey, it's just past 6.30.' He scanned the house for some recognisable sign of life.

'Look, Ira!'

The front door was opening. A tall, rangy man in jeans and a plaid shirt came out and sat in the rocker. He carried a mug of coffee. All at once Lynne was trembling. There sat Susie's grandfather.

'Let's go.' Ira leaned to open the car door for her.

Hand in hand, Lynne and Ira walked up the driveway towards the house. The man on the porch leaned forward with a look of inquiry.

'Mr Travers?' Ira asked as they approached the porch.

'That's right.' He rose to his feet.

'Mr Travers, I have something to tell you that I believe will come as a shock.' Lynne was breathless. Not from the sharp incline that brought them to the house, but with the emotions that threatened to rob her of her voice. 'I suspect Bill never told you about me. I'm Lynne Travers. Bill's wife. I mean, I *was* his wife,' she stammered. 'We're divorced.'

'Bill never said a word about being married.' Lynne recognised his bewilderment. He couldn't understand why she was here. 'But we don't hear from Bill very often.' His eyes were pained. 'But please, come into the house and meet Bill's mother.' His hand was shaking as he reached to pull the door wide in welcome. He seemed to fear that her presence meant some calamitous revelation.

They walked into an expansive living room, dominated by a stone fireplace and beamed ceilings and furnished with fine antiques.

'Please sit down,' Mr Travers urged. 'I'll get my wife.'

Lynne and Ira seated themselves on what Lynne guessed was a Queen Anne sofa dating back to the mid-seventeen hundreds. Each piece of furniture in the room bore the air of having been lovingly restored.

How was she to say to Bill's parents

218

what must be said? She waited in soaring nervousness for Mr Travers—Susie's grandfather—to return with his wife.

In a moment Mr Travers came into the room with a small, white-haired, slightly plump woman. Bill's mother must have been very pretty as a girl, Lynne thought. But at this moment her face reflected a mixture of astonishment and alarm.

Knowing she was bringing pain to this nice woman, Lynne rose to her feet and moved forward.

'I'm sorry to intrude at such an unsociable hour,' she apologised.

'That's quite all right.' Mrs Travers' innate politeness carried her through the introductions. Her husband referred to their visitors simply as Lynne and Ira. 'Fred tells me that you—that you were married to Bill.' Her eyes searched Lynne's face. She knew they were not here at this hour of the morning as tourists. 'Is he all right? Nothing's happened to him?' Anxiety threatened her composure.

'Bill's all right,' Lynne said quickly.

'Oh, I was so afraid you brought bad news. Bill never told us he was married. He's rather strange in his relationship to his father and me.' She held one small, veined hand in the other. 'Sometimes Bill is hard to understand.' Her eyes pleaded for compassion.

'Let's go out into the kitchen and have breakfast.' Mr Travers knew they were here on an urgent matter. His arm moved protectively about his wife's shoulders.

'Thank you, but we've had breakfast,' Lynne said. How was she going to tell them what was happening?

'Then you'll have coffee with us,' Mr Travers insisted. It was as though he was trying to postpone the blow of what they had to say. 'Mother makes the best cup of coffee in the state.'

The four of them walked into a large country kitchen. A round oak table surrounded by four captain's chairs with colourful, corduroy cushions sat beneath an antique lighting fixture. Mr Travers prodded them into chairs while his wife went to bring over china and silver. The atmosphere churned with unspoken revelations.

A cuckoo clock sounded, and Lynne started.

'That clock is crazy,' Mr Travers said humorously. 'It's always off time, but Mother loves it.'

Clocks were a terrifying reminder of Susie's danger.

Ira was looking at her now, his eyes urging her to state their mission. They must not waste a minute.

'I don't suppose you know about Susie,' Lynne began.

Mr Travers stiffened. His eyes moved across the kitchen to his wife.

'Who is Susie?' he asked softly.

'Your granddaughter. Bill's little girl. And mine.'

A delicate old cup dropped from Mrs Travers' hand to the floor. Her face radiated a tender joy. Her husband rose to his feet and hurried to her side.

'Bill never told us.' For the first time hostility towards his son coated his voice.

'I can't believe it.' Mrs Travers came to sit beside Lynne while her husband hid his emotions in busying himself with the coffee. 'How old is she? What does she look like?' Tears filled her eyes.

'Susie's almost five. She has long—' Lynne stopped herself. 'She has short, dark hair and blue eyes. She's adorable.'

'Lynne, you have some wallet photos, haven't you?' Ira asked. They had not given those to the vendors at the zoo.

'Yes, I have a couple.' Trying to steady her hands Lynne pulled out her wallet, flipped to the photographs of Susie. 'Here she is.'

Mrs Travers clutched the wallet in her hands. Her eyes devoured the photographs.

'Fred, our grandchild,' she said with poignant wonder. 'I thought we'd never feel that joy.' One finger lovingly brushed the small face in the snapshot before her.

'Bill never told me about you.' She compelled herself to be honest. 'He said his parents were dead.'

'Dead to him,' Mr Travers said tautly. 'Bill has no use for us. He never had, even as a child. Only for what we could do for him.'

'Fred, don't talk like that about Bill,' Mrs Travers protested. Lynne's heart reached out to the older couple. What joy Susie would have brought to them these past years. What love they could have brought to Susie and her.

'You're not up here at this hour of the morning on a sightseeing trip.' Mr Travers forced himself to be blunt. 'Is Bill causing her trouble?'

'Bill was just granted visitation rights by the courts. He has Susie for this weekend.'

Lynne geared herself to bring ugliness into their lives. 'He's been phoning me, making awful threats against Susie. Refusing to tell me where they are. I'm terrified, Mr Travers. We have to find them before he hurts Susie.'

'No!' Mrs Travers' voice soared into hysteria. 'Bill wouldn't hurt his own child. Not his own child!'

'The police can't put out an APB on Bill and Susie without evidence that he's dangerous. I'm scared of what Bill will do. I know he's psychotic.' She forced herself to continue despite Mrs Travers' agonised gasp. 'But unless we can take the police proof that he's been dangerous in the past, they can't go after him. No crime has been committed. Yet.'

'Bill wouldn't hurt his own child,' Mrs Travers reiterated piteously. 'I won't believe that.'

'Bill was a late child,' Mr Travers told them. 'Usually a late child brings joy. Bill brought only grief. We had trouble with him from the time he was three. We kept uprooting ourselves, convinced it wasn't Bill's fault. Always making excuses. He was so charming and bright. Then his grandmother died. Bill was furious that he wasn't the principal heir to her estate. The night of the funeral he vandalised his grandmother's house in rage. I can still see the devastation that met our eyes when we walked into that house.' His face was anguished in recall. 'Bill never admitted to being guilty, but we knew. Like we knew he had destroyed his grandmother's valuable doll collection earlier.'

'Fred, he was a child.' His wife pleaded for understanding. 'Bill's had years of treatment. We know that.'

'We thought he was all right,' Mr Travers conceded. 'The doctors believed he could function normally. We all wanted to believe that.'

'Bill is all right,' Mrs Travers insisted.

'Ellie, I'm sorry. We have to tell them. They have to know.' Mrs Travers broke into sobs. Her husband seemed to age as he stood before them. 'We suspect—we know—that Bill murdered five elderly women near Albany thirteen years ago. We weren't sure until the last one was killed. The police were never able to pin it on anybody, but we know.'

'Fred, no,' his wife moaned. Lynne turned to ice. *Bill was a murderer. Susie was alone with him!* 'Bill didn't do it. He couldn't have.'

'We rushed him off for treatment in Switzerland.' Mr Travers drove himself to continue. 'I sold my business so we could afford to keep him there. We retired to this house. When Bill was released, we sent him to college. We were convinced he had recovered. But Bill hates us,' he said in painful candour.

'And now he hates me,' Lynne said urgently. Bill had murdered five old ladies. She couldn't pretend Bill was out only to frighten her. Not now. 'He's threatening to maim Susie to hit back at me!'

'Mr Travers, we need you to tell the police what you suspect about Bill. Only then are they free to put out an APB to pick him up. The police will listen to his parents.'

'No!' Mrs Travers' voice was a wail of anguish. 'No. We can't accuse our son of murder! We can't be responsible for putting him away forever! You can't ask that. You can't—'

'Ellie, we have a grandchild. Think of Susie,' her husband exhorted.

'No! I won't let them put Bill away. You know what those places are like. If you talk to the police, I'll deny it. I'll deny everything.' She rocked back and forth, sobbing uncontrollably.

'Mother, you go lie down for a while.' He helped his wife from the chair and moved with her to a small room behind the kitchen. 'Lie down,' he soothed. 'We'll talk later.'

'You won't tell the police those awful things?' she pleaded through her sobs.

'I can't tell them if you don't wish it,' he told her.

Lynne turned to Ira in panic. Here was the evidence they needed. How could they make Mr Travers understand he must help them? He was their only hope.

Mr Travers closed the door to the small room off the kitchen and returned to the table.

'I know Bill should be put away where he can harm no one again.' His face was ashen. 'But I can't give evidence against my own son without his mother's acceptance. Please, give me a little time.'

'We're running out of time!' Lynne cried out. 'I haven't seen Susie since Friday evening. I don't know what Bill's done to her!'

'I'll talk to Bill's mother when she's

calmed down. I can't make this decision alone.' His pain was obvious.

'Mr Travers, if we can't bring in the police, help us find Bill ourselves,' Ira pleaded. 'Do you know where he might be?'

Mr Travers appeared to be debating within himself. Lynne's eyes were fastened to his face. He knew something.

'I don't have the right to help without his mother's consent,' Mr Travers said unhappily. 'But—but remember how Bill always hates the heat? In the summer he likes the beach.' He spoke slowly. As though talking to them in code.

'What beach?' Ira pounced.

'I can't tell you any more.' Mr Travers was upset that he had said this much. 'Not until his mother agrees.' He fumbled in his shirt pocket for a pencil and a scrap of paper. 'Please. Give me a number where I can reach you.'

Choking on disappointment, Lynne scribbled the apartment phone number on the paper. Couldn't he understand that Susie's life was at stake? How could he not help them?

'I don't know where Ira and I will go from here, but friends are standing by at my apartment. We keep in constant touch by phone.'

'I need time,' Mr Travers apologised. 'Bill's mother must understand.' He folded the paper and slipped it into his shirt pocket. His eyes were hypnotic as they held Lynne's. 'Remember how Bill hates the hot weather. He likes to be near the water in summer.' Lynne knew he was trying to transmit a clue. 'Lynne, you've given us the most precious gift in the world. Our grandchild. Nothing must happen to her.' His voice cracked. 'Find Susie.'

Chapter Twenty-Two

'What was Mr Travers trying to tell us?' Lynne asked Ira as they settled themselves in the car. 'He suspects where Bill is holed up, doesn't he?'

Ira nodded.

'He'll tell us as soon as he comes to terms with his wife.'

'Ira, we can't wait.'

'He gave us a strong hint. He thinks Bill is at some beach. He was trying to point us in a direction.'

'I've told you that Bill and I rented a cottage at Fire Island one summer. At Ocean Beach,' she pinpointed. 'And when he came to the apartment Friday evening, he said he could have been at Fire Island for the weekend. Do you suppose that's where he is?'

'We have to narrow it down a lot more than that. Does Bill know somebody who owns a house out there?'

'Not to my knowledge.'

'Did Bill ever mention another beach?' Ira pushed.

'He was furious when we couldn't rent a house at the Hamptons three summers ago—we were too in hock to afford it. I think he's gone out there with business associates.'

'Do you know where he went those times?' Ira searched for a handle.

'No. He never gave me a phone number where I could reach him when he was away. It was one of his—eccentricities.'

'We'll check with Dan and Andrea from the motel. Maybe Dan will have some idea.' Ira's face showed his frustration. 'Bill may have talked to him about some beach contact.'

'I should have made Mr Travers under-stand how desperate we are,' Lynne berated herself. 'He's our passport to Susie.'

'Honey, Mr Travers understands. But we're asking them to turn in their son on suspicion of murder.'

'Mr Travers is right,' Lynne said with conviction. 'Bill loathes the heat. He has a car. Of course he would go to some beach for the weekend.' *Which beach?* They couldn't phone every beach motel within commuting distance.

'We'll talk to Dan,' Ira said with a hopeful smile.

The town was coming awake as they swung onto Main Street. A few Sunday-dressed people were on their way to early morning church services. A jogger chugged along at the side of the road. When they turned in at the motel, further down on Route 22, Lynne saw that the Log Cabin was open for breakfast.

They parked and crossed to their unit. Ira unlocked the door, pushed it wide. Lynne hurried past him to the telephone. Maybe Dan would know a beach that Bill favoured and where he stayed when he went there. She dialled. Andrea picked up immediately.

230

'Bill hasn't phoned,' Andrea told her. 'What happened with his parents?'

'Andrea, they know he's dangerous. They suspect he killed five old ladies thirteen years ago. That's why they shipped him off to Switzerland.' Bill was a murderer, and he was alone with Susie. This ricocheted through her brain with terrifying regularity. 'So he wouldn't be caught. He was in a sanitarium for three years. They thought he was all right.' *But he wasn't all right.*

'Lynne, have them phone the Manhattan police!' Andrea's voice was electric. 'Tell them to ask for—'

'They won't!' How could they refuse when their only grandchild was in danger? 'Mrs Travers can't bring herself to turn in Bill. And his father won't do it without his mother's permission. But Mr Travers was trying to give us a message. He believes Bill is holed up at some beach. He wouldn't tell us where. Not yet—'

'Let me talk to Dan.'

Moments later Dan was on the phone.

'Andrea tells me Mr Travers suspects Bill is at some beach house?' The cool, unflappable Dan was excited.

'Yes. Do you know where it could be?'

'I have a strong hunch. When Bill's

grandmother died, she left him a beach house. I'd completely forgotten about it. Until you mentioned what his father said. I've been out there with him three times. Didn't Bill ever tell you about the house? It bugged him that the cottage was all his grandmother left him. It's a small, run-down little house in Southampton. Out of town a bit,' he corrected. 'I don't remember the address, or how to get there. Just that it's opposite a small pond.'

'Bill never mentioned it.' Bill and she were husband and wife for almost four years, but she had never really known him. 'Dan, do you suppose Bill still has the house?'

'It'll be tough to find out on a Sunday,' Dan admitted. 'Bill didn't have a phone out there. The tax records would show if he still owns the property, but the office is closed today. Wait, I know somebody who'll help.' His excitement transmitted itself to Lynne. 'Burt Winston. A fellow attorney. Most weekends he's out at his parents' house in Southampton. I'll call him, then get back to you. You're at the motel?'

'Yes.' Lynne managed a shaky smile to let Ira know there was hope.

'Stay there until I get back to you,' Dan instructed.

'Dan, wait,' Lynne said at a hand signal from Ira. 'Ira wants to talk to you.'

Lynne watched while Ira listened to Dan's report.

'Maybe we can chisel some time on this,' Ira said. 'We'll check out of the motel and head back towards New York. That way we'll be closer to Southampton if we decide to drive out. It may take you time to reach your friend. We'll check in every half hour to find out if you've learned something about the beach house.'

'Ira, I want to go to Southampton,' Lynne said when he was off the phone. She was acting on instinct again. 'Bill's there with Susie. I know that.' Every nerve in her responded to this.

'We'll go to Southampton,' Ira agreed. 'We'll pick up a Long Island map and look for the fastest route.'

Chapter Twenty-Three

'I'll go downstairs to try to reach Burt Winston at a pay phone,' Dan told Andrea. 'We have to keep this line clear in case Bill tries to reach Lynne. Got some change?' He pulled a meagre array of coins from his trouser pocket.

'I have a roll of quarters.' Andrea went to retrieve them from her purse. 'Will Burt be annoyed at your calling so early? It's barely 7.30,' she cautioned.

'Burt's an early riser,' Dan reassured her. 'He likes to go down to the beach to watch the sun rise.'

Fortified for a lengthy call to Southampton Dan sought a public phone not in use. Impatient when the nearest one was occupied, the next was out of order. He breathed a sigh of relief when the third appeared operative.

'One second,' he said when the operator asked for additional coins, and he inserted the required amount in the slot. He tapped restlessly with the fingers of his free hand while he waited for someone to respond at the other end, uneasy as he recalled Andrea's admonition about the earliness of the hour. If Burt was at the beach, he might be disturbing the elder Winstons.

'Hello.' A pleasant, feminine voice replied. A fully awake voice, his mind computed, putting guilt to rest.

'Mrs Winston?'

'Yes.'

This is Dan Watkins in New York. A friend of Burt's. My wife and I were out there with Burt one Saturday last summer—'

'Oh yes, I remember, Dan. How've you been?' Mrs Winston exuded friendliness.

'Fine, thank you.' He had no time for amenities. 'I'm sorry to be calling so early, but I'm anxious to talk to Burt. Is he up yet?'

'Burt left last night,' Mrs Winston said with regret. 'He drove out to Gurney's Inn at Montauk to consult with a client who's staying out there.'

Dan hesitated a moment, then forged ahead.

'Mrs Winston, I have an urgent problem.' He couldn't take time to explain. She was the wife and mother of lawyers. She'd

235

understand. 'I must find out if a piece of property on the edge of Southampton still belongs to a specific person. It's a life-and-death situation. Do you suppose your husband might know—'

'Let me put him on the phone,' Mrs Winston broke in. She was geared to legal emergencies. Dan heard her calling to her husband. Mr Winston had been wheelchair-bound for the past two years, but his mind was as alert as ever.

'What's the problem, Dan?' Mr Winston asked.

'We're trying to prevent a child from being maimed—or murdered,' Dan said quietly. 'I must find out if a man named Travers still owns a house near Southampton. He inherited it about thirteen years ago from his grandmother. She was a Travers, also.'

'We can't get into the tax offices on a Sunday,' Mr Winston reminded Dan. 'Let me check with a friend who's a realtor out here. He knows of every piece of property that has been sold out here for the past twenty-five years. Hold on. I'll try him on another line.'

Dan dropped more coins into the slot after the sound of a voice on the phone a couple of minutes later. He was high on anticipation. If Bill still owned the house, that's where he would be holed up. Dan would not allow himself to consider that they might be too late.

'Dan?'

He clutched the receiver with fresh tenseness as Mr Winston returned to the phone.

'Yes, sir.'

'My friend is sure that there's been no sale. He knows the property because he's tried several times in the past few years to get in touch with the owner in the hopes of listing it. The man seems unreachable. Neighbours say the house is rarely occupied. Got a pen? I'll give you the address.'

'One second.' Dan reached for his pen and pulled out a business card. 'Okay, go ahead.'

Dan hurried back to the apartment. Andrea pulled the door wide as he approached. She had heard the elevator stop at this floor, he surmised.

'Lynne just called,' she said exasperatedly. 'What took you so long?'

'Digging up information.' He pulled out the card. 'Bill still owns the house. Here's the address.'

'Oh, God, let them be in time!' Andrea spun about to face the phone. Willing it to ring.

Call us, Lynne. Call us!

Chapter Twenty-Four

Bill glanced at his watch as he layered strips of bacon across the skillet. Susie ought to be waking up any minute. If she didn't, he'd wake her. It was almost 9 a.m.

He felt great. He had sat up all night, figuring out the angles. He knew exactly how to do it. He felt a little light-headed from all the drinking last night, but he hadn't been drunk, he told himself with pride. The cold shower just now had put him into shape.

He ripped open a cylinder of biscuits and slid them onto a pan. They could go right into the oven, he gauged. Biscuits and bacon would be ready at the same time. He cracked eggs into a bowl, poured in a bit of milk, then beat the mixture into lightness.

Whistling he set the table for two. Visualising the way he'd handle it. It would be a horrible accident. An impulsive, careless little girl. He'd be the distraught father. Nobody could lay a hand on him. These accidents happened all the time. The newspapers were constantly running a paragraph or two about them.

Lynne would cry for the next fifty years. She'd never remarry. She'd never have another kid. She'd spend the rest of her life taking care of Susie. Knowing it was her fault.

The appetising aromas of bacon sizzling in the skillet and bread baking in the oven filtered into the bedroom where Susie lay, knees drawn up to her chin, beneath a plaid blanket. Christ, she looked like Lynne. He suppressed an urge to pummel that pretty little face.

Where was Lynne when he phoned the last time? Running around somewhere with that bastard Ira. Who was the chick in Lynne's apartment? No cop, he comforted himself again. The cops had no reason to stake out Lynne's apartment. He had visitation rights.

'Hey, baby—' He leaned over Susie, straining to play the doting father. 'You don't want to sleep all day.' He pushed aside the blanket and fondled her into wakefulness. 'Let's have breakfast and ride down to the beach. On the bicycle.' The charismatic Travers charm was switched on high.

'I want to talk to Mommie.' Tears filled Susie's eyes and spilled over.

'You'll do that, baby,' he crooned, hoisting her into his arms. 'We'll eat breakfast, then we'll ride down to the beach and find a phone where you can call Mommie.' He smiled cajolingly. There were no phones on the beach. They would never get to the beach today.

'You promise?'

'I promise.' He kissed her and set her down. She wasn't a little girl; she was the means of his revenge against Lynne. 'Go wash your hands and face and come to the table. Everything is almost ready. Bacon and eggs and hot biscuits. I went shopping while you slept. You like a big breakfast on Sunday morning, don't you?'

'I guess.' This morning Susie was wary.

'Go wash.' He patted her on the rump. 'After we eat, you get dressed while I bring the bike out of the toolshed.'

He turned off the gas under the bacon, drained the fat, and placed the strips on paper towelling. Now he pulled the biscuits from the oven. Still in her flower-sprigged, short nightie Susie walked into the kitchen and sat at the table. She slumped in her chair in silence while Bill scrambled the eggs.

'Sweetie, we're going to have a terrific time,' he said, shifting the scrambled eggs onto plates. 'You bring out the orange juice while I get everything else on the table.'

Make this a festive occasion, his mind ordered. If anybody saw them, let them appear a happy father with his pretty little daughter. Only his bitch of a wife and the obstetrician knew Susie was somebody else's brat.

Susie brightened as her father concentrated on creating a convivial atmosphere. After breakfast—Susie dressed now—they left the house on the bike. Susie was delighted to sit on the bar between Bill's arms. Laughing at his story about a baby chimp who loved to rollerskate.

'You should have seen this little guy. He was sensational,' Bill chortled.

The morning was cool, the beach damp.

The sun played a teasing game. Out one moment, behind the clouds the next. That was fine, Bill decided in satisfaction. That meant light traffic on the road he had chosen for the site of Susie's 'accident'.

A car would be driving away from the beach. Towards them. He would manoeuvre Susie as easily as he placed a golf ball just where he wanted it. He had this special skill. The car would mangle that pretty face. Susie would need a hundred stitches. Maybe after a dozen tries at plastic surgery she would be able to go out and have people look at her without flinching.

Bill turned into the road that led to the beach. He biked between meticulously trimmed hedges that were dramatically tall. The houses hidden behind those hedges were impressive, he conceded with envy; but it was the stretches of landscaped acreage that made them seem palatial. He craved a house like these. Right on the ocean. Stupendous views. He'd feel great in a house like that.

'Daddy, where's the beach?'

'Not far.' He was on a high. Knowing what was about to happen. Watch for a car with nothing behind it. A simple little accident with no bystanders.

Susie had to fall just the right way. But he could do it. He'd used this sensational talent of his on the golf course. In pitching a ball game. On the tennis courts. This was the real test. *He could do it.*

He didn't want her head bashed in; he wanted her face messed up. He'd position her so that her face would be at the right front wheel when she hit the road. Timing was the key.

She'd be a bloody mess, but she'd live. Lynne would want to die. She couldn't afford that pleasure. She had to live to take care of her brat.

Bill's heart pounded. His mouth was dry. His eyes were galvanised to an approaching Mercedes. Driving slowly. Nothing behind it. Keep talking to Susie. Watch for just the right instant.

Now.

'Susie, be careful!' he yelled. Loud enough to be heard by the couple in the car. He shoved her from the bar. A hand at the back of her head to thrust her in the right direction. The two in the car couldn't see. 'Susie!'

With a startled cry Susie hit the road. Her face in the path of the car's right

243

wheel. The timing was perfect. The car would graze the left side of her face. Cutting into the delicate skin. Ripping away layers.

The woman in the car screamed. The man in the driver's seat spun the wheel with superhuman skill as he ground to a stop.

'Oh, my God! You've hit her! You've hit her!' The woman was hysterical.

Susie lay immobile in shock. *The car had not touched her.* Bill swore as he jumped from the bicycle. The wheel had missed her face by half an inch.

'Baby!' Bill dropped to his haunches beside Susie. 'Baby, are you all right?'

'We'll take her to the hospital.' Pale with shock the man hovered beside Bill. The woman sat screaming in the car.

'Susie's all right,' Bill insisted. 'You didn't touch her. She's hyperactive,' he improvised. 'That's why she fell off.' He pulled her into his arms. 'Susie?' Only now did she begin to cry. 'You'd better take care of her.' Bill nodded towards the woman in the car. 'Susie wasn't touched.'

'Her face is scratched,' the man worried. 'It's bleeding.'

'It's nothing serious. She scraped it when

she fell. I'll take her home and clean it up. You didn't hit her,' Bill emphasised. Fighting to conceal his rage.

He wouldn't mess up next time.

Chapter Twenty-Five

Lynne stared at the map spread across her knees without really seeing it. Southampton was circled in ink. Dan had told Ira this was the fastest route. Instinct kept insisting that Bill was at the beach house with Susie. But they were hours away.

Her eyes left the map to read a cluster of road signs. They were only twenty-seven miles from Albany. A city that size must have an airport.

'Ira, could we take a plane from Albany to Southampton?' How long would that take? A twenty minute flight?

'We'd have to try to charter a plane,' Ira said. 'We can't waste time on that. Our safest bet is to drive straight through to Southampton.' This early on a Sunday morning traffic was light. They were hitting seventy to eighty miles an hour.

'Let me get on a phone,' Lynne pleaded. 'Let me see what we can do about a charter flight.' They'd take a cheque, wouldn't they? Somehow she'd manage to cover it by tomorrow.

'There's a gas station just ahead,' Ira capitulated. 'We'll see if they have a phone.'

Lynne was out of the car before it had fully stopped. They might be able to fly to Southampton. That would save hours. Perhaps save Susie from whatever horror Bill was cooking up.

She was running out of change. Ira bought gas and asked for three dollars in coins. She fretted at the delay this entailed. She checked with the operator for a number at the Albany airport, talked with the man in charge of charter flights. They could fly her to Southampton around six this evening. Nothing was available earlier.

Lynne returned to the car as Ira slid behind the wheel.

'I should call Dan and Andrea again—'

'You called them ten minutes ago,' Ira stopped her. 'We said every half hour.'

'If Mr Travers contacted the Southampton police, they could go right to the house.'

Desperation clamped a hand about her throat. A legal technicality stood between Susie and safety. 'The police could go to the house and take Susie. They could hold her until we arrive.'

'Honey, we'll make it,' Ira vowed. 'You believe that.'

But Bill was a psychotic who had already murdered five old ladies.

Chapter Twenty-Six

Bill hoisted Susie to the counter in the pharmacy section of the drugstore so that the sympathetic pharmacist could clean her scraped face with an antiseptic. He had remembered that the medicine chest at the house held only some used razor blades and aftershave lotion.

'It'll be fine in a couple of days,' the pharmacist calmed Susie. Gentle in his movements. 'Let's make sure we get all the dirt away.'

God, he had thought his head would burst before she stopped bawling. He had to make a show of taking care of her.

Later, if any questions came up in the cops' minds, the pharmacist would tell them how solicitous he had been when Susie fell off the bike.

At last the pharmacist released Susie. Bill bought the bottle of antiseptic and sterile bandages, listening earnestly to the pharmacist's instructions about further care. Then he lifted Susie into his arms and went out onto the street.

It was already past 10 a.m. They'd wasted a lot of time in the drugstore.

'I think you deserve some ice cream, baby,' Bill offered. 'How would you like that?'

'Chocolate chip?' Dark crescents beneath her eyes lent a special poignance to her prettiness this morning.

'Chocolate chip,' Bill agreed, and deposited her on the sidewalk. He took one small hand in his because the Sunday morning crowds were heavy. They'd leave the bike locked to the rack at the curb. 'Unless ice cream will make you cold?' The temperature was skidding downwards. The sun was nowhere in evidence. Everybody wore sweaters or jackets this morning. Nobody in their right mind would go swimming today.

'I won't be too cold.' Susie's spirits lifted. 'Where will we get it?'

'The Fudge Company. Over on Job's Lane.'

'They have ice cream at the Fudge Company?' Unexpectedly, Susie giggled.

'Oh, sure. You'll see all the fudge being stirred in the big copper kettles. Plus they've got saltwater taffy and peanut clusters.'

'And ice cream.' Susie wished for reassurance.

'And ice cream, he repeated. He'd buy her ice cream, then they'd bike back to the house. He had to figure out another plan fast. No mistakes this time. He had no time for mistakes.

They went up Job's Lane to the Fudge Company, crowded despite the early hour. They queued up to be served. At last Susie had her chocolate chip ice cream cone. She was shivering in the unseasonable chill but nibbled at the frozen concoction with enthusiasm.

I need a drink, Bill thought. A double Scotch.

'Let's go back and get the bike and ride to the house,' he told Susie. But this morning Susie insisted on dawdling.

Damn. She was freezing from the ice cream, but she had to play the tourist.

'Daddy, what's that?' She was fascinated by a pair of early teenagers posing in the pair of colonial stocks that were one of the sights on Job's Lane. Head and legs positioned in the holes of the wooden framework while a friend in high glee snapped pictures.

'Colonial stocks. To punish bad people.' Bill was short with her. 'Come on. Let's go home. It's cold.'

The temperature must have dropped twenty-five points in the past two hours, Bill thought. If he had known the weather would be so crazy, he wouldn't have come out here. But he was here, and he had a job to do.

'Daddy, you promised I could call Mommie.' Susie lifted wistful eyes to his. 'I want to call her now.'

'Finish your ice cream,' he evaded.

'I can eat it while I talk to Mommie.'

'All right.' So they'd play a little game. Bill sought a place with a phone. He dialled his own apartment in New York. Nobody would answer. He let it ring a few times, frowning while Susie waited expectantly.

'Mommie's not home.' He held the phone to her ear so she could hear the ring. 'She must still be at the beach.'

'Not at this beach?' It was a plaintive, muted wail.

'No. Mommie went somewhere else.'

Sorrowfully, Susie bit into the remainder of her ice cream. Bill pondered over what had nagged at him at irregular intervals. Had that been a woman cop in Lynne's apartment? No. He'd overreacted. Lynne wouldn't have called the cops. She'd be scared of landing on the front page of the *Daily News*. He'd dialled the wrong number both times. He was that uptight. Besides, the police couldn't get involved. No crime had been committed.

'Wait, Susie.' He reached out to stop her from walking away. 'I have to make another call.'

This time he was careful in giving the operator the number he wanted.

'That's area code 212,' he emphasised. They must have given him the wrong city last time.

He waited for the call to be put through when the coins requested had dropped into the box. He'd tell Lynne how within an hour her beautiful baby would be scarred for life. So horribly, nobody could bear to look at her. It would be like scarring Lynne.

The phone was ringing. Why didn't she answer? He tensed. Someone was picking up. He framed ugly words in his mind.

'Hello.' A man's voice replied. Bill froze. He recognised the voice. What the hell was Dan Watkins doing in Lynne's apartment? 'Hello—'

Bill hung up and reached for Susie's hand. His face was thunderous. No time to waste.

'Come on,' he snapped. 'We have to get back to the house.'

Chapter Twenty-Seven

Lynne rolled up the car window on her side. The sky was winter grey. The wind sharp. Even wearing Andrea's sweater she was cold.

'I'll close my window, too.' Without losing speed Ira managed to roll up the window on his side.

In a few minutes they would be turning

into Southampton. Lynne could sniff the scent of the ocean.

'We'll have to stop and ask directions,' Lynne reminded. *Let Susie be all right.* 'Will we be on time, Ira?' She pleaded for reassurance. Knowing that Ira was not clairvoyant.

'We will. We've broken all speed records.'

But speed records didn't count in this chase, Lynne's mind jeered. Within two terrible minutes Susie's life and hers could be wrecked.

'A storm's coming up.' Storms at the beach could be exciting. But not today.

'There's a station on the right. We'll stop and ask directions.'

Ira pulled into the gas station. He leaned out the window to question the attendant, a teenager as tanned as a lifeguard.

'I'll go inside and ask where it is,' the attendant offered, and jogged over to the office.

In moments the attendant returned with directions to Bill's beach house. Lynne and Ira listened carefully, thanked him, and moved out onto the road again.

'We'll be there in five minutes. Watch for street signs,' Ira told Lynne.

He followed directions. Driving slowly so as not to miss a turn. Lynne fretted at this enforced delay. She kept remembering the horror of Mr Travers' story about Bill and the five old ladies. Her life was in danger every day of their marriage. How could she have lived with him and not known?

'It's ten minutes,' Ira intruded on her troubled thoughts. 'We ought to be there by now.'

'We haven't come to the street yet.' All at once Lynne was panicky. 'Ira, we're lost.' They couldn't afford time.

'We'll stop and ask again. The kid at the gas station must have made a mistake.'

Ira spied a woman walking along the street. She looked as though she lived in the area. He drew up beside her, rolled down the window again, and leaned out.

'Excuse me. Could you help us with some directions, please?'

The woman walked over to the car with a friendly smile, listened to Ira's explanation about their having made a wrong turn somewhere.

'Oh, you've come down the wrong road,' she chided. 'You have to turn around and go back three blocks. Make a right at the supermarket, go down a block and make another right. It's about a mile out on that road.'

'Thank you.' Ira shifted his foot from the brake pedal to the gas.

'Ira, we can't afford these mistakes!' In her anxiety Lynne was caustic. 'Not when my baby's with that monster!'

Chapter Twenty-Eight

Bill moved from room to room, struggling with warped window frames. A gale was blowing up. He didn't need a flood in the cottage.

Part of his mind remained riveted to the memory of Dan's voice on the phone in Lynne's apartment. Lynne had phoned Dan to complain about how *he* was making threats. How did she know where to reach him? Had she remembered he lived in Katonah?

Good old Boy Scout Dan had rushed down to console her. But Dan wouldn't believe her when she said he made those threats. Dan would think Lynne was paranoid. He had the cool, lawyer's approach.

'Daddy, I'm cold,' Susie complained, drawing a folded up blanket about her small frame. 'You said we'd go swimming out here. It feels like winter.'

Bill stood frozen. Susie had just told him how to do it. Pleasure charged through him. His heart thumped in anticipation. No mistakes this time. It'd be so easy.

'It'll be real warm in here in a few minutes,' he promised. 'You know that big log by the fireplace? I'll go out to the toolshed and bring in the chain saw. We'll have a great fire going in a few minutes.'

Susie would get in the way while he tried to saw the log. Kids don't look. Everybody knew that. Chain saws were dangerous. You were always reading about some terrible accident. A leg cut off. An arm.

'You're going to start a fire in the fireplace?' Susie was intrigued.

'That's right. We'll have a great fire going in no time.' He forced himself to sound convivial.

I'll rush Susie to the hospital before she can bleed to death. Then I'll phone Lynne. She'll rush out here to the hospital. She'll be out of her mind. But nobody can touch me. Susie was a hyperactive little girl. She pushed herself in the way of the chain saw.

'Can we go out later and try to call Mommie again?' Susie asked.

'Later,' Bill agreed.

His mind raced ahead in time. He saw himself with the chain saw in hand. The chain saw whirring in frenzy. Susie screaming. It'd be just like smashing up his grandmother's dolls. It'd be like when he wiped out those old ladies who looked like his bitch of a grandmother. He'd feel sensational.

'Hey, I've got a great new game for us, Susie.' *He couldn't wait to do it.* 'It's called "Houdini".'

'How do we play it?' Susie welcomed a new diversion.

'You pull up a chair close to the fireplace. That straight-backed chair,' he pointed out. 'I'll go out to the kitchen to get some rope. On rainy days his grandmother used to set up a line in the kitchen to dry clothes. The rope was still in the drawer. 'I'll be right back.'

Susie sat in the chair, waiting for the next step in this new game. Bill returned with the length of rope. He hadn't felt this great in a long time. Swiftly he tied Susie to the chair.

'Daddy, what kind of game is this?' Now she was ambivalent.

'I told you. "Houdini". It's named after a famous man who could escape from any kind of chains or rope. I'll tie you up. Then you try to get out. I'll go out for the chain saw, and let's see if you can get free by the time I'm back.'

Bill raced to the toolshed. The outdoors was dank and chilly. The sky a murky grey. But everything was going to be fine. He'd pay Lynne back for what she did to him. He'd feel wonderful.

He picked up the chain saw and checked the fuel tank. Plenty of gas here to cut a dozen logs. Or what he had in mind for Lynne. The chain saw in one hand, Bill hurried back into the house and slammed the back door.

'Daddy?' Susie's voice was shrill. 'Daddy, I don't like this game. I'm scared—'

Bill stalked into the living room. He leaned over Susie's tiny frame. His face contorted in vindictive recall. This wasn't Susie. It was Lynne. She wouldn't be pretty with her arms and legs sawed off. She'd be a mess. His head reeled with exhilaration.

Neither Bill nor Susie had heard the car

pull to a grinding stop outside.

'Daddy!' Susie screamed as he turned on the motor of the chain saw. 'I want Mommie! I want my Mommie!'

Emerging from the car before the beach house, Lynne heard a cry.

'Ira, that's Susie!'

'Come on!'

Together they charged up to the front door. Lynne grasped the knob and flung the door open. Susie cowered in a chair. She was tied up. Bill was fiddling with the ignition on the chain saw. His objective was sickeningly clear.

'Mommie!' Susie screamed. 'Mommie!'

Bill spun around with a look of rage. Ira lunged at him. The chain saw was swept across the room as the two men struggled together. Lynne looked about for a weapon. She picked up a beat-up andiron. But she couldn't hit Bill without the danger of missing and injuring Ira.

Bill shoved Ira to the floor in animal frenzy and ran from the room. Lynne darted to untie Susie.

'Mommie, Mommie!' Susie's efforts to cling to Lynne made it difficult to free her.

'You're all right, darling,' Lynne soothed

while she struggled with the rope that imprisoned Susie.

Ira staggered to his feet and raced after Bill. She heard a car start up and speed away. Moments later another car charged behind it. Ira was chasing Bill. *He shouldn't go after Bill alone.*

'Mommie, I was so scared,' Susie sobbed. 'Daddy wanted to hurt me. I know he did.'

'It's all right now, darling.' Lynne pulled Susie into her arms.

'Stay with me, Mommie.'

'Of course, darling,' she soothed and struggled to her feet with Susie in her arms. Her eyes searched the room. Where was the phone? She must call the police. 'Susie, is there a phone in the house?'

'No,' Susie told her. Arms tight about Lynne's neck as though fearful of letting go for an instant. Then she stiffened at the sound of another car pulling up out front. 'Mommie, who's that?'

'It's all right. We'll go see.'

Still holding Susie in her arms Lynne hurried out onto the deck. Detectives spilled out of two cars. They explained that Bill's father had alerted the Southampton police.

'He's got away,' Lynne said. 'My friend went after him. They went in that direction—' She pointed. 'My friend is driving a green Dodge Spirit. Bill's in a black Peugeot.'

With Susie wrapped in a blanket and nestled on her lap, Lynne sat on the top step of the deck and watched for Ira's return. Fearful that he would catch up with Bill and be hurt. Ira was no match for Bill.

She sat still. Silently praying. Susie was safe. Let Ira, too, be safe. The two most important people in her life.

Every moment seemed an hour. Then at last she saw the green Dodge approaching. Relief lent a glow to her face.

Not moving from the step because Susie was asleep in her arms, she waited for Ira to park and come to her.

'The nightmare's over,' he said gently. 'The Travers couldn't allow anything to happen to Susie. They've given the police all the help they need to put Bill where he can hurt no one again.'

'Can the police prove Bill killed those poor old ladies?' Lynne shivered at the possibility that Bill might be freed.

'The police have finger-prints from the victims' necks. But thirteen years ago those prints checked with nothing in the police files. At fifteen Bill had never been fingerprinted.' Ira's smile was wry. 'Mr Travers pointed that out to the police. He told them, too, about the bloodied clothes Bill tried to burn in the furnace. About his knowledge of Bill's absence from the house on the night the last of the women was killed. That was the night the Travers forced themselves to face the truth. The next day they left Cranston Hills and prepared to have Bill admitted to a sanitarium in Switzerland.'

'How could I have been so blind?' Lynne whispered, anxious not to awaken Susie. 'How could I have married Bill?'

'You met him at such a vulnerable period in your life,' Ira reminded, his voice low. 'But that's all over. You'll never have to worry about Bill again. There'll be no release from an institution for the criminally insane.'

'Thank God that his parents understood.' Tears filled her eyes. 'How awful this must be for them—to turn in their own child.'

'They hope you'll let them see Susie.' Ira's eyes were questioning. 'She's very precious to them. In all this darkness she's their one joy.'

'Of course Susie will see her grandparents,' Lynne said tenderly. 'And she will love them. But I could never have seen this through without you. Susie and I owe you so much, Ira.'

'Remember, she's going to be my kid, too.' He tried for lightness. 'Together we'll help her forget all of this weekend of horror.'

'I'll be a whole person for the first time in my life.' Lynne's face was luminous. 'You, Susie, and I will be a real family.'

'Next week we'll go up to visit with my folks,' Ira said. 'They've been dying to meet you and Susie. They'll insist on a wedding up there. You won't mind indulging them in that, will you?' His eyes were gently teasing.

'I won't mind at all,' Lynne told him.

She'd thought she loved Bill. She *knew* she loved Ira.

The publishers hope that this book has given you enjoyable reading. Large Print Books are especially designed to be as easy to see and hold as possible. If you wish a complete list of our books, please ask at your local library or write directly to: Dales Large Print Books, Long Preston, North Yorkshire, BD23 4ND, England.

Other DALES Mystery Titles In Large Print

PETER CHAMBERS
Somebody Has To Lose

PETER ALDING
A Man Condemned

ALAN SEWART
Plight Of The Innocents

RODERIC JEFFRIES
The Benefits Of Death

MARY BRINGLE
Murder Most Gentrified

JAMES HADLEY CHASE
Get A Load Of This

EVELYN HARRIS
Largely Trouble

Other DALES Mystery Titles In Large Print

PHILIP McCUTCHAN
Assignment Andalusia

PETER CHAMBERS
Don't Bother To Knock

ALAN SEWART
Dead Man Drifting

PETER ALDING
Betrayed By Death

JOHN BEDFORD
Moment In Time

BRUCE CROWTHER
Black Wednesday

FRANCIS KEAST
The Last Offence

This Large Print Book for the Partially sighted, who cannot read normal print, is published under the auspices of

THE ULVERSCROFT FOUNDATION